AGENT IN PLACE

A TOM SHEPARD REDACTED MISSION FILE

PHILLIP JORDAN

FIVE FOUR PUBLISHING

Surjit,

Thanks for your continued interest in the books.

best wishes,

Get Exclusive Material

GET EXCLUSIVE NEWS AND UPDATES FROM THE AUTHOR

Thank-you for choosing to read this book.

Sign-up for more details about my life growing up on the same streets as Tom Shepard and get an exclusive e-book containing an in-depth interview and a selection of True Crime stories about the flawed but fabulous city that inspired me to write, *all for free.*

Details can be found at the end of **AGENT IN PLACE.**

Prologue

The Bedouin drew his keffiyeh headcloth tightly across his nose and pulled the brow folds forward like a visor leaving only a narrow, loose flapping slit for vision.

As the day had drawn on and the sun rose towards its zenith, the bone-dry wind that had pushed him across the plains had picked up and changed direction, lashing grains of sand into his eyes, and threatening to split the skin on his face.

Gathering the loose cloth of his traditional thawb robes about him, he clicked his crook off a loose rock and called his flock of scrawny goats to a halt.

Tethering the meagre herd of half a dozen animals, that were more skin than meat, to a stake he then took a crossed-legged seat in a shallow dip overlooking a small settlement that nudged up to the edge of the desert wilderness. Tugging the stopper from a canteen, he took a long draught, observing the trucks that had parked up on the tarmac road and the groups of men dotted around them smoking and talking. Unintelligible words and a short bark of laughter drifted to his ear on the wind. They were foreigners, marked out by language and the disrupted camouflage pattern of their uniforms.

A pickup truck kicked up a billowing dust cloud as it

approached the parked vehicles from the south. The armed men in the flatbed were Syrian, exchanging waves with the men on the ground as they passed. The rev of more engines joined the first as a column of the long-wheelbase Toyota pickups pulled in to join the trucks, each flying a large black flag, the stark white script declaring allegiance to the Islamic State of Iraq and the Levant (ISIL).

The tinkle of goats bells chimed as they scratched in the dry earth. The Bedouin fished in the folds of his robe for the small monocular that hung around his neck on a worn leather strap. He raised the lens which could be used to scour the arid landscape for strays and injured animals to instead keenly observe the convoy of vehicles and the soldiers and militiamen gathering by the roadside. A section of the latter unhitched two large fuel bowsers and began running out hoses.

The Bedouin didn't need to see the grit and debris that soiled the vehicles or observe how the soldiers' guard had fallen to weariness to know it had been a long journey. He had known they were coming and matched his pace to intercept them on this isolated patch of desert highway known as the Five Mile Market.

As the sun baked the hard-packed earth, the Bedouin focused his scope on one particular vehicle where the level of security had not slacked, the rear canvas covers remained lashed tight and a quartet of the foreign soldiers waved on any of the militia who strayed too close. Any of those who looked out from the pit stop across the shimmering lake of a mirage that rippled across the desert floor could be forgiven in thinking that was the only illusion.

Underneath the Bedouin's dusty garments was one of the United Kingdoms' most secretive operators. The man's skin, already deeply tanned from his exposure to months of desert sun, had been enhanced further with a tinted sunblock, and his hair and thick beard which had been allowed to grow unkempt were flecked with a white chalk dye.

He thumbed a small slide on the body of the monocular that launched an invisible pinpoint pulse of coded laser light at the convoy and spoke into the throat mic secured under the folds of his keffiyeh.

"Clipper, this is Neptune. How copy?"

A second later the crackled reply came through on his earpiece.

"Neptune, loud and clear. Send traffic."

"Clipper, objective identified. This a call for fire, confirm good light?"

Static hissed in Neptune's ear as the encrypted communications relayed back to the operation command centre where the duty tactical air controller would make the request from the operational command officer to engage the enemy.

"Neptune received. Stand by for confirmation."

Twenty miles west and cruising at seven kilometres above the arid rocky floor a General Atomics MQ-9 Reaper unmanned drone tilted on its axis and banked hard to port, its pilot feeding commands to the aircraft from an air-conditioned control booth nestled in a rural compound four and half thousand kilometres to the northeast in RAF Waddington, Lincolnshire.

In the pilot's headset, Neptune and the tactical air controller's conversation sounded as though the men were in the same room. He nudged the Reaper into a swooping dive and onto the co-ordinates supplied in the mission brief, settling his eyes on the diagnostic readout of the aircraft's performance, current fuel load, and ordnance status.

"Neptune. Clipper, the light is green. Confirm the call sign is Anvil. I say again, Anvil. Mark your position."

Neptune bit back the tide of adrenaline that surged up

from the pit of his stomach to throb from his temples to his toes.

Anvil was the command to strike and once again he was the tip of the spear, directing a blow against the enemy in the heart of their own territory.

Neptune was a member of Task Force Trident, part of the US-led Combined Joint Task Force which was actively engaged in assisting the Free Syrian Army and the disparate groups of Syrian rebels who were battling against their president's onslaught to hold democracy at bay, the surge of the vicious jihadi fighters of the Islamic State who had rallied to the war-torn region to further carve out their caliphate and more recently, the might of the Russian bear—the Soviet troops answering the Syrian government's call for assistance against the growing pro-democracy uprising.

Neptune reached inside the leather satchel he carried and removed and then activated a palm-sized strobe unit. The small device emitted a pulse of brilliant infrared light that would mark his position to the incoming drone pilot and aid in putting the bombs on the bullseye.

Neptune and his team from the Royal Navy's secretive Special Boat Service had been sparring with one group of ISIL militants for the past month, leaving the allied Al-Tanf airbase in their heavily armed and agile desert patrol vehicles to harass and disrupt the spirited Al-Waleed advance into the northern territories, much as their counterparts in the SAS had done under David Stirling in the Second World War.

Over the previous weeks, Al-Waleed had stepped up its campaign against the local rebel groups, targeting international aid agencies as they sought to alleviate the suffering of those trapped in the civil war, and the checkpoints of the Syrian Democratic forces, but the mercury of militancy had soared after a spectacular truck bomb attack against coalition forces near Al-Tanf and the civilian massacre of three rural villages. In a worrying turn of events, intelligence showed that the latest attacks had been aided and abetted by Russian troops.

"Neptune is lit."

"Roger, Neptune. Switch to Golf, One-Three. Your contact is Jackal One-Five."

"Neptune, switching Golf, One-Three."

The tactical air controller remained on the comm but gave over the frequency for Neptune to talk in the drone.

"Jackal One-Five, Neptune. Over."

"One-Five, awaiting check-in." The voice of the drone pilot was crystal clear, no atmospheric anomalies or technical glitches disrupting communication between the man on the ground and his RAF counterpart half a world away.

"One-Five, your target is a column of trucks two thousand metres from my mark. Two-triple-zero metres. Confirm?" said Neptune. The comm squelched as the pilot transmitted his reply.

"Two thousand from mark. Roger."

Neptune settled his IR target designator beam on the combined militant and Russian convoy that he had helped track across the desert. All the signs from the CIA's covert human intelligence sources pointed at this being a resupply and reinforcement column to establish a foothold in the battle for the north and support the ongoing enemy atrocities in the nearby city of Maghrabad but it was also highly likely they were the same troops responsible for the attack at the airbase and on the villages.

The Number 13 Squadron flight lieutenant nudged the control column to the right, dropping the Reaper drone into a banking dive on the final approach to target, and glanced down to check his armament switch selection and target information then flicked back to the high-definition screen which showed the drone's-eye view and checked that

Neptune's laser designator was illuminating the correct spot.

The Reaper's Honeywell TPE331 turboprop was closing the distance to target at just under its maximum speed of three hundred kilometres per hour, the ground closing as the pilot bled off altitude, levelling the flight as the Reaper's optics picked up the tone.

A sensor in the aircraft's nose cone detected Neptune's coded laser pulse and slewed a camera onto the target. The flight lieutenant's screen at RAF Waddington showed a clear image of the target vehicles and from the centre where his crosshairs were placed, a glowing pinpoint of energy.

"Jackal One-Five. Good light," said the pilot, flicking the switches to engage the drone's multi-spectral targeting system.

"Roger, One-Five. Confirm blue. Target remains two-triple-zero from my position you are clear hot," said Neptune.

The drone's camera had picked up and marked the flash of Neptune's strobe on the pilot's heads-up display (HUD).

"Confirm blue. Target north, two-triple-zero."

The pilot levelled the drone out at two thousand feet, confirming the status of the hardpoints holding the two five hundred pound GBU-12 Paveway II laser-guided bombs that would be released on target in less than two minutes. The target designation diamond on his HUD changed from red to green and he flicked the bomb arming sensor.

"Jackal One-Five, one minute," said the pilot, his words clipped as he concentrated on flying the azimuth line towards the ballistic release point where the weapons system's computers would calculate for accuracy and then automatically release the payload to obliterate the target.

"Thirty seconds."

Neptune hunkered into the shallow dip, far enough away to be safe from the ordnance but too long in the tooth not to be mindful of weapons malfunctions.

The goats jittered, perhaps sensing the approaching firestorm.

Neptune kept the laser designator fixed on the trucks. The Paveway's electronic nose would sniff out the coded scent of the beam and land precisely where he held the light. As he maintained focus on the weary men around the vehicles, his peripheral vision kept alert for any sense of danger to himself or changes in the scene dynamic in the two-metre square around his person.

Neptune swore.

"Neptune, all stations. Goliath. I say again, Goliath."

The tactical air controller's voice came through in a crackle, the electronics that smoothed out the speech not quite masking his tension.

"Goliath. Goliath. Jackal One-Five, abort, abort, abort."

In RAF Waddington the pilot deselected the arming triggers and fed juice to the Reaper's single engine. He heaved back the command stick and banked the aircraft hard right and into a steep climb.

"Shit," said Neptune. Shutting off the beacon and gathering his meagre belongings, he climbed to his feet. He reached out and untethered the goats, slapping them on the rump to disperse them into the desert.

The militants and the troops two thousand metres away remained in blissful ignorance of how close they had come to death, distracted now by the crowing crowd of civilians who were treading their way from the mouths of the narrow passageways of Five Mile Market with hookah pipes, gaudy fabrics, and cartons of cigarettes to hawk to the unexpected convoy.

Neptune leaned on his crook as he scrambled up a small incline and turned his back to the scene and the blazing late afternoon sunshine. Reaching the top of the escarpment, he looked back, already thinking about the next time the target would fall under his sights.

He was a killer, poised and willing to fire a bullet into the heart of his enemies. Or in this case, to let them live. That capacity for control under pressure and to adapt to rapid changes in the field was why he had excelled, first as a Royal Marine Commando and then as one of the Royal Navy's most elite operators.

He turned and scrambled down the back side of the slope, double-timing his strides across the bleak arid earth. He had a long way to go and it would be further still if he missed his rendezvous with the exfiltration helicopter that would right now be winding up to skim across the desert floor to meet him at the pre-arranged pickup in the middle of an endless dune sea.

Chapter 1

"You are wasting your time. Come here. Help me with these."

Debbie O'Connor looked into the sky. She knew with absolute surety that above the azure ceiling the satellite was there, but like everything else in the war-ravaged country, reliability was not.

"I told you not to listen to Jamal. It's too dangerous leaving the district centre." The doctor shook her head in frustration as she pushed her AK-47 personal defence weapon against the raised wheel arch of the flatbed and then struggled to heave a case of antibiotics and intravenous paracetamol off the back of the Toyota HiAce.

The journalists and photographers had a job to do, as did she. What Feriha Najir could never understand was the lengths they would go to to get a five-second piece for camera at the risk of their lives. A child knew not to stick its head in a hornet's nest. But these people?

O'Connor stowed the satphone back in its case with a shake of the head.

The cargo of the second Toyota lay in the rubble, the vials and bottles of invaluable medication exposed to the burning sun that had arrived overhead with surprising speed.

Maghrabad lay on the primary route between the cities of Aleppo and Homs and had seen itself traded off three times in the brutal civil war. The once prosperous district centre lay in ruins from heavy shelling by government forces and the subsequent counterstrikes by the Free Syrian Army and their militias in a violent, futile tug of war. Yet still, in the crumbling basements and rickety shelters of corrugated metal and fabric sheeting, those who could not leave, or stubbornly refused to, scratched a meagre and precarious existence.

Before the war, Maghrabad had enjoyed the benefit of its strategic location between the Aleppo and Idlib governorates and a once-thriving trade route with neighbouring Turkey. Now, that ribbon of tarmac road that had once been its lifeblood was a battleground as the pro-government forces pressed to encircle the north-western resistance and bring the rebellion under their boot heel.

O'Connor marked out contrails bearing north. It was impossible to tell if they were from government jets or an incursion by the pro-democracy forces trying to stave off the savage advance of the regime. The sun caught wingtips as the aircraft bore west in a lazy arc. Far enough in the distance not to be an immediate threat, but she still felt a knot of nerves. Being run to ground by indiscriminate mortar and artillery shelling was one thing. Riding out precision airstrikes was a different experience entirely.

"Here, let me help you." Debbie O'Connor leaned in to help lift a crate of baby formula out of the heat and into what was once a pharmacy. The whole building facade had gone. The twisted steel and concrete had been cleared but not removed, forming a narrow channel that blockaded the street.

"I don't know who's more crazy," said O'Connor. "I mean, at least I get paid for this."

Feriha Najir wiped the back of her forearm across her sweating brow.

"If we don't come to these people, they die." She shrugged, picked up another holdall of dressings and tossed it into the shade.

O'Connor looked at her watch.

"They should be back by now." A wariness was creeping into her tone.

"Yes. They should. I have patients and I can't do all this shorthanded." Najir pointed at the sacks of grain and water. "Can you set that up over there? I want them to come through the clinic before they take the supplies."

O'Connor set to the task, feeling guilty. A distant bombardment had awoken them before dawn. Encamped five miles from the weekly rendezvous to serve the populace of Maghrabad's Fourth and Fifth Districts, they'd had an elevated view of the column of technicals and larger armoured carriers that rolled west into the neighbouring town.

Ian Reardon, her photographer and cameraman, had persuaded her to let him get closer and capture the assault in the hope of some much-vaunted shots of Russian troops supporting the Syrian militia in their cleanse. Reardon and Jamal had left before the sun was up. O'Connor grunted as she heaved another sack onto the pile. They should have been back.

Each sack bore the crescent and the cross of Dawa lil'Abria, the non-profit agency that funded and enabled Feriha Najir's small ragtag army of volunteers on the ground to provide food, medicine and care to those trapped by the fighting. A poor man's Red Crescent but providing welcome relief along the stretched front and the outlying regions and governances. The support paled against the challenge faced by humanitarian organisations along the border routes as tens of thousands fled the bloody war and sought safety and shelter in the sprawling encampments springing up daily.

"Here they come." Feriha poured water over her hands and dried them with a clean rag tucked in the front pocket of her dusty jeans, shading her eyes as a small family broke cover of the shattered factory across the street.

"As-salaam 'alaikum." She called the greeting as one of the small children broke free of his mother's grip and charged across to leap into her arms.

"Feriha. Feriha. Feriha." His face was broken in a broad grin.

"Qasim, come here. Leave the doctor be. Apologies, Doctor Najir."

Feriha waved the apology away and ruffled the boy's hair.

"No need. I'm just glad my assistant has come so early. I think I'm going to need a lot of help today." She crouched and smiled.

Qasim looked at her with a smile that reached his ears. Feriha stood, embracing his mother and offering a brief bow to his father, who had the same grin as the boy but weary eyes.

"Sabbah, Feriha." Professor Kamel Shami reached out to shake her hand. "Every week, he can't wait to see you. I think he has a crush."

"Baba!" Qasim admonished, slapping the hand away as it gripped his shoulder. Shami laughed, which turned quickly into a harsh cough.

"You are well?"

"We are surviving."

"I have medicine for the cough, but you look skinny since I last saw you. Go through. Abdullah?" Feriha called into the back of the pharmacy, visible through a gaping hole where a cluster bomb had opened the wall to the rear compound. "Abdullah, we have guests."

A shout of acknowledgement came from behind a split oil barrel. Flames danced under blackened steel where charcoals heated a tin of roasted potatoes and green beans. The scent of spices and fat filled the air.

"Maryam, how is baby?" Feriha patted Qasim on the head and shooed him towards O'Connor who was lifting the last of the sacks into the shade. The boy scurried off, greeting the Irishwoman with a bear hug. Prising the child off with an equally enthusiastic welcome of kisses, she produced a sneaky bottle of Coca Cola from the top of an upturned refrigerator and passed it over.

"She has been grizzly. I think she's teething."

Feriha looked into the swaddling. The baby's eyes screwed shut and her nose wrinkled, saliva drooling from the cute pink mouth which reached out for the tip of Feriha's pinkie finger.

"I can give her shots today and I have some gel to take with you. Give it to her when they are irritating her. Your parents?"

Maryam Shami's face clouded. She eased the child in her arms to a more comfortable position.

"My father stays today. It's harder for him and it's far. My mother wouldn't leave him."

"Arthritis," said Kamel.

"I'm sorry. I could try to get someone to deliver across town?"

"No." Shami shook his head. "It is too dangerous. The militias are running rampant along the crescent parkland. They have the support of the Russians now." He shook his head sadly.

"We heard them this morning. To the west."

"And the north," he said.

Feriha glimpsed more people threading their way on foot through the blockade towards the small clinic. Her team of a dozen volunteers broke from their cover of shade to offer welcome with a cool drink and begin the triage of injuries and illnesses that preceded the simple warm meal of vegetable and potatoes and to issue some staples to see them through until the next week.

In the distance, the whine of a revving engine echoed off the ruined walls.

"I don't have many anti-inflammatories, but I'll give you something to take back. Will you not try to go for the border?"

Kamel Shami looked across to Qasim as he helped O'Connor distribute the sacks of grain and rice into smaller bags.

"Maryam's parents are too weak for the journey. Maybe at the end of the month. The Wolves are running trucks to Nusaybin. In the meantime, her brother watches over us," he said.

Too weak and too proud. Feriha understood the predicament. From Byzantium, generations of the same families had farmed, laboured and toiled the small region and those with the sense had put personal safety over personal history. Now, for those who remained, it may be too late.

The road from Maghrabad to the Turkish border and the camps at Nusaybin or Kilis was treacherous. Civilian traffic had dwindled to nothing. Anything on the road was easily targeted by the opposing sides and it was an odyssey by foot. By day refugees would face the brutal sun and by night the freezing winds that whipped across the desert plain bringing plummeting temperatures.

She knew that The Wolves of the Western Resistance were shuttling those who wished to take their chance seeking asylum in the convoys that collected arms and ammunition from the US-backed amalgam of Free Syrian militias and the altogether more shad-Turkish Peshmerga groupings. It was a gamble. But then so was staying put.

"Debbie! Feriha!" The shouts were faint and followed the roar of an engine and the dull thunk of undercarriage meeting rock.

"Feriha!"

Najir recognised the voice. Reardon.

She quickly waved the Shamis into the shade of the building and stepped out into the street. Jamal's Nissan pickup steamed water and oil from the engine block. The rear passenger tyre flat.

"Feriha. Help us."

Ian Reardon leapt from the driver's seat. He was six foot, with a day's stubble on his chin having abstained from his ritual shave to get on the road early. A brown and white keffiyeh flapped loosely around his neck, and his khaki cargo pants were stained with blood.

"Ian... Ian!" O'Connor ran up behind Najir as Reardon dropped the pickup's tail lid, hauled Jamal out, and propped him against the rear wheel.

"Christ." O'Connor dropped to her knees and helped Feriha as she cut off Jamal's shirt. Blood bloomed from his upper right arm.

"Leave him," said Reardon

"He's been shot, Ian," O'Connor shouted. "How bloody close did you get?"

"Close. Very close. Feriha, come here. Quick."

Reardon had pulled himself into the flatbed of the Nissan and dragged a torn piece of hessian sacking to the lip.

"Who is this?"

"They were fleeing the shelling. We had to help." Reardon opened his arms. A shrug of hopeless choice.

Feriha climbed in and then ushered Reardon back.

"Why did you bring them here?" She pointed at the two patients.

"They need a doctor."

"They are dying."

"I know."

O'Connor stepped up on the wheel arch.

"Stand back, Qasim," she said.

The boy in the back of the Nissan wasn't much older than the inquisitive child, and the man may have been his brother or father. Both complexions were a shade of yellow. The whites of their eyes had haemorrhaged red and vomit stained their faces and clothes. Limbs and hands twisted in acute rictus.

"What is wrong with them?"

"Gas? Chemicals? I don't know. The bastards shelled the entire village. There were hundreds of people in the square," said Reardon.

"Get me water," ordered Feriha. "Rinse their eyes and mouths and then douse them before you strip them. Debbie, get yourself gloves and a mask." Feriha pulled a pair of scissors from her pocket and cut the tee shirts of the two victims vertically. She shrank back. The skin of their chests was blistering. Gathering her composure, she cut two small squares of the cloth and stowed them in one of the small sample vials from her vest kit.

"Abdullah…"

She heard the screams just before the distinct sound of rifle fire.

The people who had come for medicine and sanctuary scattered. The roar of fifty calibre weapons boomed in the distance, a dust cloud rising above the dozen or more technicals, the black flags with white inscriptions prominent as they bore down Al-Sulaiman Road.

"Qasim!" O'Connor jumped from the wheel arch and grabbed for the child as the wave of panicked people threatened to stampede over him. She pulled him close as shouts and screams rose around her.

Reardon grabbed her arm and dragged them through the melee to the lee of the old pharmacy.

"I have it, Debbie. I have it all on camera. I got the

bastards."

In the midst of the chaos, he was smiling. Triumphant.

Then came the blood-chilling whistle of incoming shells.

Chapter 2

The dust storm that blew across the landing zone at Al-Tanf blotted out the sun and disrupted the state-of-the-art communication array, peppering the huge disk with thousands of minute particles of sand and fine desert dust.

"Pirate-Four-Five, Clipper. Go, Olive-one, two." Clipper, call-sign for the Tactical Air Controller (TAC) dialled in the frequency and clamped a hand over the earpiece of his headset to better block out the storm that battered the Joint Special Forces Command Centre.

The reply was preceded by a static squelch.

"Pirate-Four-Five. Roger, Olive-one, two. Clipper, we have a mass of armour and equipment twenty clicks from zero. Civilian population centre under fire, request weapons free."

Squelch.

"Clipper, wait one, Pirate-Four-Five." The TAC looked over his shoulder and turned in his chair.

"Colonel. Incursion Six, Seven, Charlie, October. Pirate-Four-Five has a column of armour and civilians under fire. Request weapons free."

Colonel Duncan McPeak strode over to observe the screens.

"Captain Stevens."

"Sir?"

McPeak was greyhound thin, with a narrow mouth and a preternatural ability to monitor the dynamic shifts on the battlefield. He pointed at the map as he spoke.

"Six, Seven, Charlie, October. That's east of the MSR outside Maghrabad. Reaper Nine tracked a column last night seventy clicks south-east of that. Could this be the same troops?"

Stevens studied the ground.

"Possible. A dozen technicals backed by armoured personnel carriers. Local and irregular troops travelling under ISIL flags. Intel identified them as part of the Al-Waleed militia."

"Irregular troops? We just keep it simple and call them Russian in here, Captain Stevens," said McPeak. He cocked his head as he viewed the battlefield, mindful of the stakes and the multitude of pieces in play.

"Al-Waleed have been making land gains for the last month and Trident have been skirmishing with a company-sized contingent of Russian troops along the edge of the fifty-five for weeks." He noted the demarcation of the fifty-five-kilometre deconfliction zone around the Al-Tanf Air Base, an area designated to ensure there were no international incidents sparked by the US and her allies engaging with the Russian troops supporting the Syrian regime's advances into the northern territories but which was fast becoming the frontline in a dangerous game of cat and mouse between the sides.

"If they're shelling a civilian centre, it's a problem."

"Danny, can he confirm belligerents? I can't risk letting him engage if this is the Western Wolves and a bunch of local Al-Waleed fighters giving each other the finger."

Danny Wallace keyed his comms.

"Clipper. Pirate-Four-Five."

"Pirate-Four-Five, send."

"Four-Five. Request visual confirmation on targets. No contact at this time."

"Copy, Pirate-Four-Five. Standby on visual."

"Danny, where are Coyote?"

"Returning to base."

"Have Four-Five hold high on overwatch and re-task Coyote. Let's get a better look at who we are hunting." McPeak sat down on his khaki fold-out chair behind the TAC and they waited.

Chapter 3

"...Deborah O'Connor, for NR News International. Maghrabad."

O'Connor held her grim face until the spotlight died and Reardon gave her the thumbs up.

"Got it," he said.

"Okay. Have we time to package it together and get it away?"

Reardon pulled the memory card from the Nikon and slotted it into his MacBook. A few clicks and the files began to transfer.

"Should be fine. How's Jamal?"

O'Connor glanced across to the corner of the old building where Feriha Najir was thumping a shot into the driver's arm.

"I'll go see. Tell me when that's ready. Do you have the satphone?"

Reardon nodded, and she patted his arm.

It had been close.

The rubble and the natural barricades that had formed along Al-Sulaiman Road had stalled the militia's initial lightning advance. Toppled buildings, burned-out vehicles, and the craters left by incoming ordnance, hindering speed and aggression across the ground.

The crowds had scattered like geese; those who broke cover and ran across the main road, cut down by long-range gunfire from the technicals. The others fleeing into the shattered buildings now faced being hunted down by the troops who had disembarked and were sweeping the district centre on foot.

Feriha had been her usual decisive self and that had saved the journalists, the young boy, and his family.

As O'Connor and Reardon had taken Qasim and sheltered in the pharmacy, the doctor had leapt into the Toyota, gunned it to life and slewed into the rear compound. Abdullah, under her instruction, loaded the Shami family into the cab. The journalists climbed onto the flatbed, flung against each other as Reardon snapped off shot after shot of the ensuing chaos.

The lane from the back of the pharmacy followed the edge of an old repair shop and electronics factory, eventually turning into one of the less damaged main roads that led to the Al-Suft roundabout and the ring road. Feriha pushed the Toyota at breakneck speed until she took the off-ramp and descended into a neighbourhood of low-rise shops and flat-roofed apartments. They decamped the vehicle in a garage and had set up in the temporary shelter of the business it once served.

"Is he going to be okay?" said O'Connor.

"He will survive the wound. Will he survive the day? I don't know. What was he thinking?"

Feriha jabbed a finger at Reardon, who was bent low, face illuminated by the laptop screen.

"He was doing his job."

Feriha shook her head, eyes screwed shut in fury.

"He has condemned us to death so your viewers can be entertained over their dinner."

"We're highlighting the injustice here, Feriha. We're on your side."

"My side? My side? If you were on the side of these people, your country would be doing what they did in Kuwait. In Iraq. Afghanistan." Feriha spoke in a whisper through gritted teeth, her eyes on Qasim peering from under his mother's protective embrace. "Instead they are playing politics while your countrymen watch mine die on TV and do nothing!"

"That's not fair, Feriha. We're making sure people hear the truth of what is happening."

Reardon turned from the laptop screen.

"Those two people from the village. What was that?" he said.

Feriha tilted her head away from Jamal and the family, huddled on cushions left behind by the owners in their haste to leave. Better to spare them any more fear than that which already gripped them.

The humidity spilled in as Feriha shoved the broken door open and stepped outside. Reardon pulled a pack of Lucky Strike from a breast pocket and offered them around.

"I don't know. Chemicals. Gas. You were there, what did you see?" Having accepted a light, Feriha took a long draw. She folded her arms and stared down the barren street. A dog slinked between buildings, ducked its head and sniffed the air, then relieved itself on the rusted wheel of an abandoned car.

"We got as close as we could and took the rise overlooking the village on foot. The militia were a couple of kilometres east. We saw a car leave the village and head out. I don't know if the Muezzin had been told to gather everyone in the square, but it was packed."

Reardon blew a stream of smoke into the air.

"Then they just opened fire. A barrage of rockets. Whoever left in the car had the place zeroed because the first rockets landed right in the centre of the crowd."

"They didn't explode?"

"Yes and no. People fell. I've photographs of horrible injuries. Within minutes, people were foaming at the nose and mouth. Convulsing. I could smell something. I want to be more specific, but I don't know." He shrugged. "Vinegar. Rotten eggs. Barbecue gas?"

Reardon took out another cigarette and lit it with his first.

"I'd caught it all on camera when we spotted the motorbike. When we got to them they were suffocating. I didn't know what else to do but bring them back."

"They wouldn't have survived anyway."

The trio looked to the west from where they had left the two bodies in the back of Jamal's Nissan.

"We need to move again. Those troops must have seen you and followed you back. They'll be searching."

"I'm sorry, Feriha."

The doctor nodded. Patted the man on the arm.

"I know you are. It's this shitty war." She shrugged and turned back inside.

The wash of the explosion threw her fifteen feet across the room. Dust, glass and rocks followed the door and window as the shop front was blown in.

"Feriha!"

The panicked shouts of Jamal and the Shamis sounded miles away from her ringing ears. Debbie O'Connor lay two feet away, blood pouring from her nose and mouth, a deep laceration running from her temple across her forehead.

There was no sign of Reardon.

Kamel Shami dragged the Irishwoman to her feet, guiding her towards the back of the small space. A dull crump and a second explosion rocked the building, plaster falling from the ceiling as the mortar shell overshot and exploded on the roof of the building next door.

Feriha Najir shook the concussion of the blast from her

head. Abdullah was helping Jamal to his feet. His words lost. Wild gestures to get out. Feriha felt blood trickle from her ear.

Dust from the impact was clouding the room. She pulled the shemagh around her nose and mouth, choking up a cough.

O'Connor was breaking down the laptop and camera.

"Leave it." Feriha grabbed the woman by the arm and dragged her towards the steps to the garage.

The journalist shook her off.

"We need to get this out."

"Ian is dead. We'll all be the same if we don't move." Feriha grabbed her again.

"Help me."

The doctor swore but grabbed Reardon's camera case and the satphone as O'Connor bundled a selection of cables, USB chargers and the laptop into her rucksack.

They followed Abdullah into the basement.

The Toyota was wrecked. The first blast had caved the roof in. The bonnet was buried, and the windscreen crushed. The steering column twisted uselessly against what remained of the dash.

"Into the alley," shouted Feriha. She ran to the bed of the truck, reached into the exposed bed and pulled out the AK-47.

Abdullah half carried, half dragged Jamal out and into the narrow passage that ran along the back of the shops, the Shami family in tow. O'Connor exited next, chasing the family up the alley. Qasim broke free of his mother's grip to run back towards her.

The mortar landed ten yards ahead of Abdullah.

O'Connor threw herself over the boy.

The concussive wave lifted Feriha from her feet and slammed her over the top of an industrial steel waste bin. She landed heavily on her back.

"Debbie? Qasim?" Feriha pushed the bin and the covering of food waste out of the way, scrambling into the cloud of dust to follow the sound of choking coughs.

"Debbie?"

O'Connor had the boy wrapped in her arms, but he was dead. Her left leg was twisted unnaturally under her and blood drooled from her mouth.

"No. No. No. No..." Feriha dragged the journalist's shirt up, but shrapnel had torn into her tummy and torso. Blood was pumping out of the wounds.

"Feriha..." O'Connor's words were weak. She reached out to shake the Syrian doctor off her.

"Feriha. Don't waste your time. Go."

Feriha lifted the woman's arm. A long sliver of metal had penetrated the armpit and was poking through the pectoral muscle above her breast.

"Feriha. Take this. Make sure someone sees it." O'Connor grabbed the doctor, staring grimly into eyes filled with tears. O'Connor nodded, seeking confirmation, her head lolling on an unsteady neck.

"Debbie."

"Get out of here." O'Connor shoved the rucksack containing the laptop and her report alongside Reardon's images into Feriha's hands with the last of her strength. A final smile and then she closed her eyes.

Chapter 4

"Two builders and a spicy chai."

"Gash, you're in the wrong game, mate. Cheers."

"You're in the wrong bloody outfit. Spicy chai? Catch yourself on, Token. No wonder your own lot left you behind."

"Fuck off. Puddle pirates, the lot of you. It's as well you've a proper hooligan in this squad or we'd all be stuffed."

Corporal Andy Moore took the spiced tea from his oppo, Corporal Gareth Day.

Equal in rank and training but as far apart as sky and sea. Moore was former Parachute Regiment and Day a Royal Marine Commando. The nickname bestowed on the former by his band of brothers was due to him being the only man of green army descent in their joint special forces patrol.

"Where's the boss?" said Day.

"Pissing off the Yanks." The third team member took a long slurp of his tea and two sugars, narrowly avoiding the barriers as he raced a Lamborghini around the Nürburgring, head weaving left and right as he manoeuvred around each corner. Without taking his eyes off the screen or his hands from the controller, he raised an elbow towards the window and the large hangar beyond that housed the helicopters of the Special Forces Aviation Wing.

"You still trying to beat my time, Sarge? Give it up. Lewis Hamilton couldn't catch me on that."

Sergeant Mark Mills ignored the jibe and concentrated on getting the big Diablo back on the tarmac.

The unit's small rest area comprised a plastic patio table and four chairs, a low slung sofa that had been inherited from the last rotation and still bore the battle-damage, a forty-inch television propped on an old ammo crate and a PlayStation.

The boss's corner of the room had a reclining La-Z-Boy sofa, a selection of the day's newspapers and a box of paperbacks. A locked filing cabinet held the standing orders and any other admin the team needed to go about their business: Meal and ammo chits, copies of identification, and next of kin arrangements.

Mills was another Royal Marine, both he and Day and the patrol's captain, Tom Shepard, having earned the coveted green beret on completion of Royal Marine commando training at Lympstone in Devon had then gone on to endure the rigours required to be badged in the Royal Navy's elite Special Boat Service. Token had followed his own course from Aldershot to Stirling Lines in Hereford.

The men now operated together as part of the UKSF assistance to the Syrian Democratic Forces and Free Syrian Army.

"Captain Shepard?"

"Who wants to know?" said Token, placing down his mug and rising to face the newcomer.

"O-Group in ten. Colonel McPeak's orders." The lance corporal was a wiry Scot and new to country given the extent of the sunburn on his cheeks.

"He's in the hangar. I'll let him know."

"Cheers, Corporal."

"What's doing?" said Day over his shoulder.

"Something's going on in Maghrabad. Heard they gassed a village this morning and the TAC are saying Al-Waleed and the Russians are in contact in the town. Could be the rebels need a bailout."

"Fuck off," said Mills, dropping the controller. The team had been harassing the Al-Waleed militia for weeks, their last skirmish ending in a vicious exchange with an enemy later identified as irregular Russian Spetsnaz.

"Gospel." The LC put up a right hand.

"Much obliged but you can piss off now. Big boys work to do." The NCO exited as Mills flicked the TV off.

"Token. Go get the boss. Gash, let's get the gear stowed. If the kid's on the level we'll be up for this one."

❖

Tom Shepard cycled the last three reps of the barbell overhead and then dropped it in the dirt, pausing its bounce with a foot before racing to the big tractor tyre. He hooked the makeshift harness over his head and flicked out the chains. Fighting the weight from a dead start into a slow walk, he got the tyre moving then settled into a powerful run along the sandy track that now separated the hangar from the airstrip following the earlier storm. The hundred-and-twenty-kilo tyre bobbled behind, friction and every bump in the course threatening to stall forward momentum. His thighs and lungs burned as he drove towards the end of the thirty-metre pull to the midpoint; to another heavier barbell and then the tyre drag back to the finish proper.

He could hear the ragged breath of the 160th Special Operations Air Regiment (SOAR) pilot not far behind him. The heat of the morning sun made the physical battle tougher than it needed to be. A pair of Apache gunships swooping in to land proved things could always get worse.

Shepard stumbled a half step, throwing up a hand to protect his eyes from the downdraft of the two taxiing attack choppers. The dust storm filled his nose and mouth with sand causing him to lose valuable momentum and struggle to get the tyre back up to speed.

Lieutenant Karl Cochrane close behind let off a string of expletives in his Texan drawl. Shepard gritted his teeth and drove the last few steps, dropping the tyre.

"The only easy day was yesterday, Corky," he said, chest heaving, the red welts of the harness scarring his torso.

"Fuck you, Paddy." Cochrane slumped onto his haunches as he dropped his tyre, sucking in deep breaths.

The roar of the Apaches drowned out the whoops and catcalls from the other end of the track. Mechanics, crew and few of the division's SEALs on downtime watching the Brit take on the elite US pilot.

Shepard gripped the second barbell and heaved it from ground to chest to overhead, then let it drop.

Twenty-nine to go.

"Boss!"

Twenty-eight.

Cochrane had grabbed his own barbell.

Twenty-seven.

"Captain."

Shepard could see a commotion at the spectator end. Picked out the antagonist. Shit.

Twenty-six.

"Tom."

Shepard dropped the bar.

"Piss off, I'm winning here, Andy."

Twenty-five.

"Ah shit. Heads up, lads." Token took a step away from the two competitors.

Shepard and Cochrane dropped their barbells at the same time.

"I have people tell me you are the extension of my arm; the scalpel I'm to wield to cut the insurgency out of this shitty cancer of a civil war and give what's left back to the people who deserve it. But do you know what? You're Neanderthals. It's like letting a fucking bricklayer do the job of a brain surgeon." The woman's hair hung loose and whipped around her face as the Apaches slowed and finally parked. She pinned the blonde strands with a pair of Ray-Ban aviators. Cocked her head at Token.

"Corporal."

"Ma'am."

"You here to get these monkeys to my meeting?"

"What are you talking about, Porter?" said Shepard, hands on hips and competition forgotten at the sight of the Special Operations Group intelligence officer.

Christmas Porter shook her head.

"O-Group in five. Try to spruce yourselves up a bit first, though."

She nodded at Moore and angled off towards the JSOC.

"Do I sense some chemistry between those two, Corporal?" said Cochrane, wiping sweat from his eyes.

Token grinned and jerked a thumb over his shoulder.

"It's not those two you should be thinking about, LT. Word is Ivan's been playing with his whole bloody set."

Chapter 5

The dull rumble of the BTR-82's engine reverberated off the corrugated wreckage of the factory roof, the ragged and less-well tuned growl of eight Toyota Hilux technicals adding a percussive beat from where they formed a loose semi-circle closing off the end of the road to any of the crowd considering escape.

"These people are doing you no favours." Dimitri Yegorov stood in front of the mass of huddled captives, the low cries of a baby and short whimpers of the frightened the only response to his words being translated into the local dialect by a masked militiaman standing behind his left shoulder.

Yegorov waved away the flies that tried to settle. A city of ten thousand reduced to mostly wreckage and rubble, combined with the heat and bodies buried beneath, created a fertile breeding ground for the swarms that plagued the survivors. For the Russian, the pests were a constant reminder of the nuisance the Western Resistance was causing; holding him back from the cities of the south to assist the ragtag and volatile militant groups and inept regular militia who had repeatedly failed to break the north-western uprising.

"They call themselves the Wolves of the West, but they are

frightened dogs. Why else would they abandon you here? To starve and to listen to the lies of the desperate Americans. Leaving you to answer for their criminality while they hide among you, putting your children, your families in the firing line." The Russian looked along the faces. Most avoided his gaze. Those who didn't either frightened or hostile.

"Your president needs support. Your help in bringing these murderers to heel."

A whimper rippled through the masses as a group of militia, faces wrapped in black shemagh, appeared on the parapet of the factory roof. AKM carbines aimed down into the crowd.

"Look at this! Baby formula. Medicine. Coca Cola." Yegorov kicked over the stack of supplies that his men had dragged from the front of the pharmacy. "Who brought this here? Who buys your silence?"

No answer. Eyes in the dust. The swirl of sand and clunk as the door of the BTR opened and a stocky soldier exited, carbine slung over his shoulder and Makarov pistol in hand. He marched to the colonel and handed over the sidearm.

Yegorov nodded and two militiamen grabbed a man and a young boy from the crowd. The wail of women and angry shouts of the men rose but aggressive commands from the soldiers and the points of their AK-47 rifles restored a modicum of order. Any further dissent was quashed at the ratchet of eight DShK heavy machine guns being cocked in the beds of the technicals.

The two stumbled, feet scrabbling for traction as they were forced forwards and deposited six feet from Yegorov.

"Who among you is with the resistance?"

The man stared at the ground defiantly. The boy was in his early teens and the whimper of a mother or sister sounded between wider words of support.

"We know the West-loving dogs are here. They tried to

help these two terrorists." He pointed at the two corpses dragged from the bed of the wrecked Nissan and laid out in the street.

"You. Speak." He pushed the boy into the dirt.

"Who here thought to harbour this scum?"

No reply.

Dimitri Yegorov sniffed. Cocked the Makarov.

"Ali!" he shouted, looking to the rooftops. One fighter nodded. He disappeared briefly then a scuffle sounded, the voice of protest. On the roof, the fighters pushed six men towards the edge, hands tied behind their backs with plastic zip ties, rudimentary nooses of rope around their necks.

"Yallah." The colonel chopped his hand down.

The six men scrambled for purchase on the parapet but it was futile. Cuffed and overpowered, they were flung into the air, their fall arrested after a few feet by the jar of the tightening ropes.

The crack of a neck robbed Yegorov of one example, but the rest gave him the grisly spectacle he sought. Dancing feet, twisting bodies, life slowly choking out in full view of their peers and community. He raised his hand and clicked his fingers.

The boom of the mounted DShK guns was deafening as they opened up on the struggling prisoners. Capable of rattling off six hundred rounds a minute, the barrage was over in less than six seconds.

The 12.7x108mm cartridges scythed through flesh and bone, cutting the victims from their ropes and dropping them into bloody heaps against the footing of the building.

Yegorov put the pistol to the boy's head and pulled the trigger. The spray of blood and brain matter washed across the kneeling man's face. He collapsed, heaving, onto the ground. Yegorov pulled him up by the collar. Face to face. Blood dripped from the man's chin.

The Russian's tone was like flint. "Where are they hiding?"

Chapter 6

Feriha Najir scrambled up the escarpment of concrete blocks and twisted pillars and climbed onto an exposed balcony. Two gaping holes in the exposed bricks looked out across the city where the windows had once been.

She flinched at the sound of heavy machine-gun fire nearby. Falling over the sill and tangling in ripped curtains, she fought rising panic and tugged the barrel of the AK-47 free of the material's grasp. She was soaked in sweat, stained with Debbie O'Connor's blood, and stressed. She dropped the rifle and slid against the back wall, knees pulled up to her chest, glad to be in the relative cover of the apartment, but still too close to her pursuers.

The screams carried on the wind through the derelict concrete canyons and she knew it was only a matter of time before they crushed the resolve of their prisoners and found someone willing to speak about the doctor who brought Western aid and access to the caravans north and west. If she was unlucky, they would already know she offered assistance to any fighters who found themselves injured in the battle for freedom and democracy against the tyrannical regime and that they could find her in the east market.

Feriha dug in her pack for a bottle of water. Draining most of it in three gulps, then pouring the rest into her hands she scoured the dust and grit from her face; scrubbing away the grief for Qasim, his family, and the journalists. There would be time to reflect later. To feel and to process but right now she needed to move. She needed help.

The apartment had been her bolthole for a month now and while it was convenient and situated strategically at the converging access points between the freeways and the central run into Al-Sulaiman Road and the city, it now felt exposed and anything but secure.

The crump of mortar rounds made her jump as she hoisted O'Connor's rucksack onto a table. Unfastening the drawstring and pulling out the journalist's MacBook, she thumbed the power button, watching with growing anxiety the slow scroll of the progress bar across the screen. The password button appeared on the background of a desert sunset. Feriha typed Debbie O'Connor's last words into the window.

A chime of success and the desktop appeared. She shook her head. Just like Reardon. Icons haphazardly dropped, no sense of order to the files. Using the touchpad, she opened the recent document finder and filtered by date. The last file held several documents and MPEG video files. She clicked the first Word doc.

An avalanche of stones skittered and tumbled down the front of the building followed by another burst of heavy gunfire that sounded much closer than before. Feriha pushed the laptop lid halfway closed and crossed the room. Straining her ears, she plucked the rifle from the floor and eased to the edge of the window. Another shower of stones from above. Reflexively, she ducked back into cover. The sun reflected off the lintel, heat radiating inwards as though from an open oven door. Najir eased the curtains aside and peered out to the street below.

An explosion of movement and piercing ambush of sound

ricocheted around her face. She stumbled back from the window, the curtains flapping wildly under the assault. Feriha losing balance fell to her backside, rifle clutched tight against her chest. A yell of surprise. Heart racing. The equally startled pigeon flew a circuit of the room with a series of frightened hoots before finding the shattered skylight and exiting into the city, a fan of feathers drifting to the floor in its wake.

Feriha lay still, bringing her breath back under control. She stood, battling the anxiety and fear coiling around her. She opened the laptop again, glancing around for invisible intruders.

O'Connor's document was a succinct version of her last piece to camera, redone for print outlets. It detailed Reardon's video and stills showing the village assault. Militia cutting off the egress routes and detailing unidentified military support units. Reardon's excellent long-range work picking out Caucasian faces and Russian military equipment. Feriha clicked the first MPEG.

The camera was shaky to begin; Abdullah's feet in view as they crested a hill. The ground was rocky, desert scrub growing out of the broad cracks in the parched earth. Reardon moved behind a broad fan-shaped rock and settled the camera on the village, the lens taking in the gathering community before drifting to the east and a column of men and vehicles.

She flinched as the first rockets fired. Heard the distinct whump, whump, whump, whump as they left the launchers in a flash of flame and smoke, the distant screams and panic as they landed in the crowd. The camera lingered on the carnage, picking up Reardon's and Abdullah's shocked commentary as the camera panned across. Shrapnel injuries. Stampede. The flailing futility as people fell under the crush and the choking yellow-green mist. Reardon panned to the west.

A group headed by a cropped-haired white man wearing a grim smile observed the slaughter through field glasses. A blur of the camera tightening and then the clarity of focus. At the same time, the binoculars dropped, and the face turned to a local militant. Snapping back east with binoculars raised to stare down the barrel of Reardon's camera. Lips moving. He dropped the glasses to his chest and gestured at the vehicles around him.

Reardon's camera shifted then picked out a small cloud of dust leaving the village. A heartbeat later the focus blurred, the camera's motion frenetic as the rocky ground erupted in gouts of incoming fifty calibre gunfire.

Feriha Najir released a breath. She scrubbed back the video, the faces in shot as familiar as her own reflection.

Khalid Al-Salam, self-styled Emir of Daesh in the Western Provinces. Responsible for the murder and maiming of thousands under his flag of twisted hate. Principle orchestrator of the kidnap and torture of anti-establishment figures, foreign journalists and charity workers. Al-Salam was the Jack of Clubs in the hierarchy of targets within the vicious Al-Waleed network the special operators of the Combined Joint Task Force had been hunting for the last eight months since a convoy of British Red Cross volunteers had been massacred.

The man to his right was equally reviled in the region. Colonel Dimitri Yegorov, 21st Spetsnaz Brigade and commandant of the Russian spearhead into the annexation of Crimea before his deployment to help undermine the Arab Spring sweeping the Middle East. The colonel's orders as part of a GRU black-bag team were the removal of dissenters and spokespersons against the faltering regimes before the Russian Federation accepted the government's request for direct military aid. Yegorov had then been deployed with a brigade of his men to reinforce and help take back territory from anti-regime forces and the Free Syrian Army. His means to do so had been as swift and ruthless as the Daesh blitzkrieg three years earlier.

Feriha Najir had been digging for information on their movements and networks for the last twelve weeks in a bid to stall the advance against her allies in the Western Wolves Resistance, the doctor's mission to bring aid to the people, not her only aim. Supporters of the regime change offered observations and titbits of local knowledge, information she fed back to her handlers so that a larger tactical picture could be painted and appropriate action taken. She looked at the carnage in the village, took a sample vial of the chemical compound from the clothing in her pocket and looked at the two small squares of fabric. She knew that Reardon's recklessness and his recordings may well have tipped the scales if the evidence made it out of the city. Chemical attacks by government forces weren't new but hard evidence had always been elusive. With this, international outrage could well force a temporary Russian withdrawal and perhaps push for full coalition involvement in the battle against the president and his hard-line policies.

"Feriha!"

She slammed the laptop closed, snatched the AK-47 from its sling and took aim in the caller's direction, finger tightening on the trigger, the weapon arcing up towards the figure in the doorway.

"Feriha! It's me. Reza."

"Reza!" Feriha swept the barrel wide. "What are you doing? I could have shot you!"

"What's that?" He nodded at the laptop, O'Connor's stuffed rucksack of notes, Reardon's camera, and the satellite phone beside them.

"Nothing to concern yourself with." Feriha shoved the

MacBook into the pack.

Reza Yousef stepped closer, dark eyes narrowing as he watched her pull the drawstring and secrete the plastic sample in her vest.

"Feriha, we need to get you away from here. The Russians are everywhere. Al-Salam's men are sweeping the northern quarter and they are moving to cut off the freeway. We have to move."

She swore to herself. If Al-Waleed and the Russians blocked off the main road, a run through the city would be protracted and dangerous. She needed to get O'Connor's report out.

Yousef pushed a thumb over his shoulder.

"Come on. I have transport. We can make the interchange of highway sixty and the four-nine-nine. Ibrahim's men are coming to get us."

"They're coming?"

"We got word of the raid on Misraa. My people saw the column hit the clinic but had to stay back. I called him when I found out. Give me the gun." The younger Egyptian émigré twitched his fingers.

"You're not armed?"

"I couldn't risk the streets with a weapon. The militia and the army are all over the place. Come on, give it to me. If we run into a patrol, I'll hold them up while you run for the highway." He looked down again at the rucksack. "Whatever is in there, it looks like you need to get it to Ibrahim."

Feriha hoisted the pack and gripped it tight against her side. Although Reza was right, and while she also concluded the evidence needed to get out, she wasn't sure handing it over to the rebels would have the greatest impact. Once she was out of the city, she could reassess. The Egyptian fixer took a step forwards.

"We need to hurry." He held out his hand. Feriha unslung

the Soviet rifle and handed it over.

"Okay. Let's go. How far away are you?"

"Not far. The gardens by the mosque on El-Jabal," said Reza.

Feriha knew the spot. Another block of shattered apartments and a once-thriving community of shops and offices around a square of shaded grass and pistachio trees. The mosque's facade was riddled with small arms fire but miraculously untouched by the bombing.

Reza slung the weapon over his shoulder and reached out a hand, clasping her arm.

"I'm glad you are safe, Feriha."

The doctor nodded. Another crump of mortar fire left her feeling anything but.

"Let's go, Reza. We need to get out of the city."

Chapter 7

The wash of air-con was a welcome break from the baking sun as Tom Shepard and Mark Mills entered the Ops Centre.

The O-group was set up around a strategy table behind the bank of manned communications gear and monitors displaying the feeds from Al-Tanf's drones and surveillance aircraft traversing the skies above and around the Joint Coalition Airbase.

The heads of state were already there and in deep discussion.

Colonel Duncan McPeak, with a cup of steaming coffee to his lips, listened as his XO Captain Stevens prodded a large map with a finger. Christmas Porter stood to one side, shaking her head while Lieutenant Haley Adams of the Joint Special Forces Air Wing (JSFAW) offered a shrug. Shepard liked the pilot. She was as consummate a pro as he had encountered in his career so far. Cool, calm, and collected under fire and could put her bird over a target in a firefight or a sandstorm as though she was dropping off a band of holidaymakers. The shrug could have been taken as cockiness, but Shepard read it as an easy confidence he knew had been honed in conflict. Adams' path from an East End London sink estate and a childhood in the care system to the pinnacle of military aviation had been a tough one, but the challenges had sharpened the young woman's abilities to a razor edge.

Shepard's superior and OC of Task Force Trident offered an observation which seemed to agree with Adams' attitude of ambivalence. He nodded as the two SBS operators joined them.

"Captain Shepard. Sergeant." Major John Canning stepped aside to allow the troopers a better view of the object of discussion.

"Glad you could make it," said Christmas Porter. She uncrossed her arms and took a sip from a water bottle.

"Happy to be at your service, Miss Porter."

"Okay, you two, knock it on the head," said McPeak. The relationship between Task Force Trident and the head of the intelligence branch had been prickly of late.

Porter's informants and web of human intelligence had been incredibly successful in identifying persons and locations of interest for Canning and Trident, however, the last three serials had been hard fought, flawed, and unnecessarily dangerous. Three of the team had been shipped back to Turkey for treatment of wounds, and Shepard was vocal in the debrief that the intel sources had become more interested in their payday than the accuracy of their information.

Porter, with her usual sangfroid, had offered her own perspective on Shepard's recklessness and questioned his ability to adapt on the ground which had led to pointed fingers, caustic exchanges, and Shepard accusing the HUMINT of deliberately setting up an ambush to double their income. Since that incendiary meeting, Canning had managed to keep the two apart.

Stevens' insistence they were both in the Orders Group meeting meant whatever was to be discussed was likely going to be significant.

"You haven't missed much, Captain Shepard. This morning at oh-eight-hundred, Pirate-Four-Five was on combat air patrol when he made a request for weapons free on a column of vehicles and personnel due east of Maghrabad." He tapped the map. "Misraa. Not much of a strategic significance, but it is a stronghold for fighters of the Western Resistance in the region now larger parts of the city are beginning to fall to the enemy. We considered it a low-grade scuffle between the Wolves and a contingent of Al-Waleed and then this happened. Corporal?"

The TAC nudged his mouse and launched the review screen of Pirate-Four-Five's digital joint reconnaissance pod slung underneath the AV-8B Harrier ground attack jet. The 8042 sensor and Vigil's super IR feeds offered high-resolution tactical recon imagery of Misraa and the western plains as the jet traversed above at a height of eight kilometres.

The footage showed Four-Five performing a long, slow arc across barren terrain then, as the population centre neared the DJRP's sensors and cameras, caught the action on the ground.

"BTRs and technicals. Since we missed that chance to hit them with an airstrike the Russians have been giving Al-Waleed a major boost in pushing further north for weeks but what's with the stand-off? They usually just steamroll in?" said Shepard.

"Danny." Stevens nodded at the TAC and a separate set of forward-looking infrared cameras came online.

"Coyote Six and Nine. AH-64 Apache Longbows. Six miles out. Keep an eye on the left of the shot in two."

The two gunships hugged the dunes on approach. Rocky river beds and wadis flashed by as their two General Electric T700 turboshaft engines rocketed them across the desert at close to four hundred kilometres per hour, the camera flaring as they performed a ninety-degree turn and dropped into a hover on the edge of a rocky ridge. The TAC's integrated speakers replayed the comms.

"Coyote Six, in position. Confirm Nine. I've got visual at eleven. Do you have sight of target?"

"Copy Six. Confirm visual. Thirty-seven hundred metres."

"Clipper. Six. Personnel and vehicles grid Six, Seven, Charlie, October. Ah, Clipper, be advised column are not friendlies."

"Six. Nine. Clipper. Confirm hostile?"

"Six. Clipper. Roger. Al-Waleed banners. Visual on six, make that seven technicals and one APC."

"Clipper. Hold one."

"Coyote Nine. Clipper. Update last. We have a GRAD in area. Repeat. Rocket system moving in target area."

"Clipper. Coyote. Received."

The comms chatter lit up as the truck-mounted multiple rocket launchers fired on the village. Shepard tuned out the Coyote's commentary, focused on the lazy arcs as the rockets found targets.

"Yegorov?"

"Likely," said McPeak. "Similar battle orders. Hit hard. Hit fast. This one though has given us a twist."

"Jesus." John Canning hissed a breath as the Apache's imaging systems picked out the devastation in Misraa Square.

"No sign of HE." Mark Mills shook his head. "Dirty bastards."

"Chem?" said Shepard.

McPeak drained the last of his coffee and placed the mug on the edge of the TAC's desk.

"We have to assume so from the footage. There's no way, given the position of dominance they hold in the region, we are going to secure the site and get independent inspectors in without turning it into a pitched battle."

"The fuckers are going to get away with another massacre

then are they?" said Mills.

"Sergeant?" Canning warned.

"It's okay, Major. He's only saying what we are all thinking." McPeak held up a palm to stave off an apology from the trooper.

"So you need us to go in and do the boffins' jobs for them on the QT?" said Shepard.

"Bit more complicated than that, Captain."

Shepard looked at Major Canning, who offered nothing. Mills was engrossed and appalled at the lack of action being taken on the column of vehicles outside the dying village, given the ordnance available by fast air and from the twin gunships within three miles of this new ground zero.

McPeak gestured to the Special Operations Group intelligence officer to take front and centre.

"Christmas, why don't you give the gentlemen the good news first."

Chapter 8

Avenue Eleven ran parallel to the residential area where the safe house was located. They had exited discreetly out the rear of the building and followed yet another abandoned rubble-strewn street until they turned into the avenue, Reza leading the way with Feriha on his heels, walking quickly so as not to draw immediate attention to themselves should wary eyes be watching.

Approaching the end of the avenue and its intersection with Risha-Omar Street, they diverted through the shattered facade of a once-thriving café. Hookah pipes and upturned tables littered the small shop. Shattered tea glasses and mosaic tiling crunched underfoot as they squeezed behind the counter and into the prep area to exit out the rear door into a rubbish-strewn alley, the minarets of the El-Jabal Mosque visible in the distance.

"You're sure Ibrahim will be there?"

"Yes," said Reza, as he heaved an industrial waste bin out of the way, the screech of metal setting Feriha's teeth and nerves on edge.

"What is in your bag, Feriha?"

"It's not mine. It belongs to the journalists."

"The Irish? Where are they? Fled back to the Americans to

leave us in the shit again?"

"They're dead, Reza. I need to return this equipment to their people."

"What?" Reza paused. Looked at her and then at the bag.

"Dump the bloody bag, or keep it and sell what's in it."

"I can't. It's important."

"Important enough to get us killed?"

Feriha didn't reply. She peered into the sky, a blue ribbon threading the high walls and roof parapets of the alleyway, ears alert for the telltale buzz of a drone. The Russians didn't risk ambush or snipers by putting boots into this shattered no man's land without a flyover first.

"Is that why they are hunting you?"

"Who says they know anything about me?" said Feriha. The deaths of the Shami family and Debbie O'Connor were weighing on her. Reardon and Abdullah, not so much. Torn over what their recklessness had unleashed, but buoyed by the evidence she held.

"I'm not stupid, Feriha. I see the look on your face." He turned away, took a few steps. "It doesn't matter. You must tell Ibrahim anyway. He won't risk you bringing Yegorov to his door."

"I'll deal with Ibrahim. Let's just get as far away from here as we can."

The Egyptian scowled and stomped off. Feriha hitched the pack to a more comfortable position and considered her options. There was no way around what was coming and she hoped the hot-headed Ibrahim could be persuaded to see the value in the action she needed to take and understand it was for the greater good.

They approached the El-Jabal Gardens from the north, entering under a high stone arch and weaving along dry bark paths towards the mosque on the eastern corner. Outside the house of worship, bumped up on the kerb and obscuring the front door, was a white box van.

Reza pushed the doctor into a grove of olive trees, shading them from the sun and any keen eyes. The two watched and waited for a few minutes.

The van wasn't running, but the rear brake lamps glowed and the tinny sounds of the stereo filtered across the street and into the gardens. There was no immediate sign of Ibrahim or his men.

"Come on. They must be inside." Reza pushed up from his crouch and, ensuring Feriha was following, they exited under a second stone arch and ran across the deserted street.

"Shit!" Reza crashed to a sliding halt against the railing that skirted the mosque.

Feriha stared at the cab.

The blood of the occupants coated the windshield, the driver's head lolling to one side, passenger slumped over the dash.

The driver's side window was shattered and the door panel peppered with high calibre bullet holes. From the look of it, they hadn't stood a chance.

"Wait!" Reza pulled her back as she reached for the door.

"It could be booby-trapped. Leave them, they're dead."

Feriha peered into the cab. The driver was definitely dead. The lower half of his jaw was missing and a stitch of bloody impacts from throat to navel had taken his life. The passenger was slumped forwards, eyes still wide, flies feasting on the blood of a single neck wound. His hand rested on the stock of an AK-47 he had not been able to bring to bear. Neither man was Ibrahim.

"Let's get inside." Reza led the way up the steps and through the archway below the minaret.

The doors to the wudu were open a crack, and he pushed on the right leaf with the barrel of Feriha's assault rifle.

While the outside of the house of worship was relatively

unscathed, the inside told a different story. Shoes littered the covered walkways, and the once polished marble of the ablutions was smeared dark with grime and blood. Like everywhere that had seen death, the flies had taken over. Feriha rested a hand on Reza's shoulder as the two crept beyond and inside the prayer hall. When the first government attacks had hit the quarter and the roads and hospital had been put out of action, the El-Jabal Mosque had become not only a place of sanctuary but a triage and emergency centre. All that remained of that panicked and gory first wave were the prayer mats that lay scattered amongst the leftover field dressings, bloodied stretchers made from bedsheets and curtains, and the personal items of the dead.

Slumped against the minbar with his throat cut was Ibrahim.

"Reza, who else knew he was coming here?" Feriha left the Egyptian and moved to assess the leader of the Western Resistance fighters.

"Don't..."

"I know. I'm not stupid. Who knew?" She waved off the grab and assessed the body for traps. Confident there was none, she rolled him over. He was stone cold, his shirt front soaked in blood, and a grotesque second smile had been cut across his throat to mirror the first. His pistol remained secure in the holster strapped to his thigh.

"I... I don't know who he told but he might have organised a bolthole if we got trapped in the city or asked for more help. If he did somebody could have talked. " The Egyptian clutched the AK to his chest, eyes darting around the high arched windows.

"Feriha, this is a trap."

Feriha Najir looked at the corpse of the man who had fought long and hard for the cause of democracy. He hadn't deserved to die like that. It hadn't been a soldier's death.

They had murdered him. Cut him down like a sick dog.

She pulled the Makarov PM pistol from the dead man's holster and dropped the magazine. The pistol was the mainstay of the Syrian Army and the clip was full. She racked the slide and chambered the first of the eight rounds then pushed the weapon into her vest.

"Reza, I need you to cover the door."

"What? Feriha, we have to get out of here!"

"I can't do that."

"We need to get out of here now. What are you talking about?"

"The journalist's kit. These." She drew out one of the plastic sample vials. "I need to get these to someone."

"Who? Ibrahim is dead. We are alone. If we go quick, we can make the sewage tunnels and lie low until nightfall. When Ibrahim doesn't return the Wolves will send others. It will be easier after dark."

"No it won't, the militia and the Russians will have drones up and we'll stick out like balls on a bullock. Besides, they won't send anyone else until they work out why Ibrahim hasn't returned. Watch the doors. We aren't going to the tunnels."

"Where are we going then?"

Feriha unslung O'Connor's pack and set it on the floor. Tugging the ties free, she pulled out the bulky satphone.

"Feriha?" Reza stared at her.

"We're going to the overpass on the four-ten. It's open ground, but there are buildings underneath and to the edge to hide in while we wait."

"Wait for who?"

Feriha thumbed the power switch and looked at the Egyptian. They could debate her duplicity once clear and away and the evidence of the Misraa attack was in the hands of those who knew what to do with it. She started as a voice came on the line.

"State your authorisation code, please."

"November. Golf. Zulu. Nine. One. Echo. Eight."

"Authorisation confirmed. Please state your request."

"This is Kestrel. Request immediate extraction. Repeat immediate extraction. Grid Sierra Ten-Seven. Designate Hotel One-One."

"Kestrel. Confirm. Standby."

The line went dead and then a series of clicks pipped. Half a minute passed.

"Kestrel. Condor. Are you okay?"

Feriha's contact sounded breathy. Caught unawares and called in haste.

"I need pick up. Myself plus one."

"Are you compromised?"

"Not directly."

"Either of you injured?"

"No."

"What happened?"

"There was an attack on an outlying village."

"Misraa?"

"Yes. I have evidence."

The line went quiet. She could imagine the calculations and the conversations taking place a few hundred kilometres away.

"Proceed to pick up."

"How long?"

"We'll be as quick as we can."

Chapter 9

Shepard stood on the apron of the JSFAW landing pad and checked his watch. The team were well within the sixty-minute standby for launch. Nearby Token, Mark Mills and Gash were undertaking the routine business of checking kit fresh from the quick battle orders brief.

On the fringe of Mission Support Station Sinbad, Haley Adams and her co-pilot were walking around their big Merlin doing the pre-flights. The crew of the smaller second bird in the line did likewise. The Lynx would carry a backup crew of four including the two SBS snipers of Task Force Trident to offer overwatch, the helicopter holding off at altitude to give Corporals Crossan and Heath the widest area possible to cover with their 7.62mm L96 rifles.

Across the strip, Karl Cochrane and his crew were following the same routine on the US HH-60 Pave Hawk which would provide airborne Command and Control with Major Canning aboard. The 160th SOAR chopper would be a passive observer on the mission, monitoring the moving parts but also, if required, providing additional fire support from the twin-door mounted chain guns and mobilising and directing the QRF from Al-Tanf should they be compromised on the ground.

The thirty-minute standby could come at any second. From

there they would load up for a cockpit standby and then rotors turning standby. It was a formality after that.

Adam's Merlin would airlift Shepard with his team to the exfil location dubbed Hotel One-One on the overpass of Highway 410. The three-lane interchange had enough room for the Merlin to approach from the north and touch down, allowing Shepard's team to secure the cargo and then bug out. Time on the ground would be less than seven minutes.

"How reliable is she?" said Shepard, securing his H&K 9mm USP to the front of his vest.

"Golden." Christmas Porter tucked a strand of flyaway blonde hair behind her ear.

"You'll forgive me if take that with a pinch of salt."

"Do you know what your problem is?"

"I'm sure you're going to tell me."

Christmas Porter batted away a barrage of dust flies.

"Forget it. You're not worth the aggravation."

Shepard smiled. A small victory over the intelligence officer. He returned to checking the spare magazines. His vest and hip webbing held half a dozen black Magpul PMAGs, each holding forty AR-15 .223 rounds for his main assault weapon, the Colt L119A2 carbine.

"Kestrel is solid," said Porter. "She provided the lead on the Quala AW arms dump and put together the package on Warlock."

Shepard nodded. He thumbed power to the Trijicon ACOG sight then drew a bead, ensuring the red dot aim-point was active. He looked back to the intelligence officer.

"Intel was tight on those, Porter. It went to shit after that though."

Porter rolled her eyes. "Different source. You're supposed to train for the unexpected anyway."

Shepard ignored her, thinking back to both of the previous raids. The groundwork had been impressive. The raid on the

Quala District Al-Waleed cell had recovered twenty-one Russian-made anti-personnel devices, a hundred and fifty sticks of dynamite and nine thousand rounds of ammunition. Porter's source had uncovered a militant cell in the midst of stockpiling for an attack on Al-Tanf and coalition support structures in the city of Maghrabad. Several weeks of recon at great personal risk had pinpointed the cache to an exact location. Ops like Quala usually had the team rolling through the night, kicking down doors and clearing safe houses in a general area until they found the goods. Precision intelligence saved lives. The longer Shepard and the squad were on the ground, the higher the chance of counter-attack and nobody wanted to be stranded in Maghrabad and caught in a running gun battle.

The second op to target Warlock was another coup. Al-Waleed's accounts emir funded the local militia groups and financed weapon procurement and operations against the Free Syrian and coalition forces. Aside from the munitions, the Quala raid had recovered hard drives and mobile phones but it was Porter's boots on the ground that had narrowed Warlock's safe house down to a compound of four business units on the western fringe of the city's industrial centre. His itinerary being plotted to the second enabled Shepard to lift the man without a shot fired.

"Now she's in the shit. I guess we owe her."

"I'd prefer to keep her in theatre, but if she has evidence of the Misraa attack, we need her out."

"She say who the plus one is?"

"No. I'll put money on resistance. She wouldn't have called an extract unless she was desperate."

"I don't like mystery passengers, Christmas."

"Tie him and bag him. He won't be much of a problem then. Are you getting squeamish on me?"

Shepard scowled and bit back a response, knowing the

barb was to provoke. Porter and her Special Activities Division and Special Operations Group were the snatch squad. Trident had their hands free for the minute, but they were soldiers governed by convention. Porter operated somewhere in the shade of grey where rules rarely applied or were rewritten to suit.

A squelch interrupted on Shepard's SELEX earpiece.

"All call signs. Trident. Cockpit standby. Final check for go."

"Got to love you and leave you, Porter." Shepard whistled across at his squad, but the three were already on their feet. Each man running a last check over the kit of the man in front. They wore an eclectic mix of mismatched BDU uniform but each had a standard loadout. Ballistic helmet with integrated SELEX comms and a pop up/down bracket for night vision goggles (NVGs) they wouldn't need. Elbow and knee pads, carbines slung across chests, and pouches stuffed with spare ammunition and grenades. Mills favoured a similar chest rig to Shepard for his USP, while Gash and Token had their pistols in low-slung thigh holsters. Gash also carried a Mossberg 500 tactical shotgun and Token an M72 LAW, light anti-tank weapon.

"Shepard, be careful."

He turned back to Porter, a wry grin breaking his bearded face.

"I thought we were expendable?"

"You are." She dropped her aviators over her eyes. "I just don't want to have my guys get hurt if they've to go in and bring your body back."

Shepard shook his head and made to move. Mills was aboard the Merlin and hauling Token up by the arm.

"Yegorov is a nasty bastard."

"I've overheard you calling me worse than that in the mess, Porter."

"Listening into private conversations? I'll make a spook of you yet." Porter gave a broad grin.

"Get in and get out, Shepard. No fucking about. Even if Yegorov lifts his head high enough for you to give him a bloody nose now isn't the time." Porter pushed her hands in her pockets as the whine of the Merlin's rotors started up.

His SELEX squelched again, Adam's voice edged in static and the background hum of the rotors coming up to idle.

"M-Bad Air Six-One. This is a final call for all passengers on today's flight to Hotel One-One. Can all frequent flyers, loyalty card holders, and old ass frogmen please come forward now for boarding…"

Shepard looked to the cockpit. Haley Adams had her visor dropped and her wrist up to the windshield, tapping her watch. He raised a single finger in salute.

"We know our job. I'll have your girl back before you know it."

"Stick to the mission parameters this time. No surprises." She turned on her heel and walked towards the ops room.

Shepard stared after her for a second. The American was a master at getting in the last word.

Chapter 10

"What is kestrel? Tell me what is going on, Feriha?"

Reza Yousef had paused again; leaning against a sheet of rusty corrugated iron erected to serve as a deterrent against looters. It hadn't worked and they had stripped the small grocery store of provisions. Shelving units, lights, and even the fridges had been removed though the items were useless now since reliable power had been cut by shelling six months earlier.

"I'll explain later. We have to keep going."

"I'm not going anywhere unless you tell me.."

"Reza!" Feriha spun on the smaller man. "Ibrahim and his men are dead. We are lucky whoever did it moved on and we have a way to get out of here…"

"But…"

"But nothing. Move. We have another six blocks and we need to be ready when they arrive."

"When who arrives?"

Feriha sighed and walked away. Who indeed? she thought. Apart from the first meeting, her contact with the coalition forces had been indirect. Snatched calls on a satphone and occasional burst transmissions on an old Lenovo laptop running a cutting edge encrypted chat programme which required a complicated 3G link. She had no scruples about what she'd been doing. Spying. Ibrahim's ways may have had merit, but they did not always align with those who had a greater plan in play. While she regretted the times she'd offered up a resistance operation, she knew it was for a greater good.

The raid on the Quala weapons dump was one such of merit. Ibrahim had been content with a truck bomb that would have obliterated the militant cell but ended any chance of a lead on Warlock and the intelligence Feriha's handler could extort from his capture. Walking under an old archway that blotted out the sun, she shuddered at the thought of the trials she had imposed upon the man and offered a silent prayer that her own reckoning for her part in his pains would be many years away. She was at once without regret, but also at odds with her oath to heal.

The dynamics and the duplicity had been put on the table of the old tea shop on Al-Hataab Street, the American woman's blonde hair secreted under a wig and the pale material of her hijab as she passed herself off as a Dawa lil'Abria resource manager. Feriha knew straight away the truth of what was being asked of her and she accepted the risks without hesitation.

Kamal-Kayali Alley opened onto Al-Yasmeen Road and two blocks across the concrete ramp of the 410 overpass rose above the low flat roofs of the shops and dwellings and the small square of elm trees and low benches. Checking over her shoulder, Feriha made sure Reza was following. The Egyptian was, albeit with a morose expression and a languid gait.

She paused at the edge of the alley. The road in both directions seemed deserted. Wind whipped dust and broken rubble from the ground and into the neck of her shirt and her eyes, leaving them uncomfortable and gritty. As Reza nudged up beside her, for one instant in all the months of her undercover work, she felt the overwhelming desire for security and a long hot bath.

"I think it's clear. I'll go as far as the elms and then I'll cover you."

Reza didn't speak. A single nod in return. She could understand his reticence. She had the same feeling when he arrived at the safe house.

"We'll be safe soon," she said, clasping his shoulder and offering a smile of confidence that she didn't feel.

She was an asset in a war zone. An agent in place. At the mercy of her enemy and the whim of allies she didn't really know.

Chapter 11

"Rickshaw One-Four. On approach. Visual on Hotel One-One. Two thousand metres."

"Gauntlet. Roger, One-Four. Clear to proceed. Gauntlet taking orbit Fox-Nine. Buzzard, eyes on One-One. Confirm LS is clear." Major Canning's clipped orders directed the Lynx to advance to the landing site.

From his position on the left side of the Merlin's fuselage, Shepard watched Cochrane's HH-60 peel away and take a high banking turn to the command position Fox-Nine.

"Trident. Fifteen hundred. Doors are clear." Haley Adam's voice crackled over the comms.

"Roger on doors," said Shepard. He eased across the benching and grasped the release, pulling the handle and pushing the door out onto the airframe.

There was a sudden pressure change and a howl of wind ripped through the cabin as Token did the same on the opposite side.

"Sixty seconds."

"Roger. Sixty seconds," said Shepard, the vibrations of the Merlin's engines and the thrum of the rotors distorting Adam's time check in the SELEX earpiece.

The bird bounced on an updraft of air and he tightened his grip on the grab handle, leaning out the door to look ahead at the wide concrete berm of the lanes rising to the interchange. The ruins of the city rushed past below. Ahead, the roadway tapered into gridlock. Abandoned cars and vehicles littered the verges and central reservation.

"Clear left."

"Clear right," echoed Token.

The Lynx chattered past at pace. Crossan and Heath dangled from each side, legs buffeted by the wind, and searching the landing site for targets. The Lynx banked away, and the Merlin descended fifty feet below the snipers.

"Buzzard. LS. Confirm clear. Repeat. Good for touchdown."

"One-Four. LS on nose. Flare for landing in thirty…"

"Gauntlet. One-Four. Visual on two, repeat two bodies leaving underpass. Buzzard. Check two."

"Buzzard. Roger. Two. One male. One female. Gauntlet. Confirm Kestrel."

"Kestrel. Kestrel, copy over." Canning's voice buzzed across the comms net, patched back to the ops room where an interlink afforded air-to-ground communication.

Shepard watched as the man raced to keep pace with the woman running ahead up the steep bank of the pass. He stopped twice to glance behind and then up to the approaching helicopters, AK-47 gripped tight, finger on trigger as he weaved between the wrecks of cars and rubble.

"Trident. Small arms. Buzzard copy."

"Got him, Skip." Crossan's voice confirming he had the weapon covered.

Shepard watched the woman take a knee beside a white box truck, the cab burned out, the truck collapsed on flat tyres and ruined suspension, blocky satphone pressed to her ear.

"Kestrel copy. Ready for extraction."

"This is Gauntlet. All call signs, go for pickup. Buzzard. Eyes peeled."

"Buzzard. Copy."

Haley Adams keyed back the big turboprops, and the airframe of the Merlin screamed as power bled off and the nose flared for landing.

"Clear. Clear. Clear." Token fed his right-side observation over the net.

"Roger. Clear left, Haley," said Shepard. The ground was rushing up to meet them now.

"Shit. Contact. Left, left, left. One hundred metres. Vehicle on the move."

Shepard watched an old silver Peugeot 308 bobble over the uneven ground and swerve between obstructions as it headed up the ramp.

Kestrel popped her head around the truck. Her compatriot ducked behind the twisted curve of the damaged central impact barrier.

"One-Four. Final approach."

"Buzzard. One-Four. Single vehicle. No visual on occupants."

"Trident," Shepard broke over the net. "Hard stop. Hard stop."

The boom of Crossan's L96 cracked over comms. Shepard watched two rounds slam into the engine block of the Peugeot. The car slewed and crunched against an abandoned taxi.

"Two hundred metres." Haley Adams called out the closing distance.

"Guns. Guns. Guns." Crossan's warning came through clearly as the rear doors of the car opened and two men leapt out. Standard local loadout of AK-47s. The first man dropped behind the car, raising his weapon at the circling Lynx, the barrel illuminated with muzzle flare, casings spilling over and off the bonnet.

"Buzzard. Taking small arms fire."

"This is Gauntlet. Free to engage."

Crossan's sniper rifle barked again. The militant flew back, a 7.62mm bullet ripping through his chest cavity.

The second man sprinted forwards, firing from the hip at the approaching Merlin.

"One-Four. One-Four. Abort. Abort." Canning's voice was followed by a squelch of static.

Shepard watched as Kestrel broke cover and fired off four rounds at the running man, diving back behind the metalwork of the van as his aim changed and impact sparks started dancing off the ground and cover of the vehicles bodywork. Shepard was slammed into his harness as Adams shoved power back to the engines and heaved the cyclic.

"Contact. Second vehicle," Token shouted.

Shepard spotted the flatbed pickup, three men in the rear.

"RPG. RPG," he called.

Shepard freed his rifle and leaned into the airframe, dropping the sight over the second vehicle which dipped and bucked as the Merlin banked away from landing.

He squeezed the trigger. Popping off rounds. The vehicle wildly slewing through the obstacles.

Kestrel had moved; her compatriot running to join her when Token called it.

"IED!"

The approaching gunman was running, slaloming around the burned-out van and weaving between the cars that had collided with the central barrier.

"Buzzard. One-Four. Break. Break. Break."

The militant made a last leap across the reservation and detonated his vest.

The shockwave bucked the Merlin. Shrill warning tones blared through the cabin and Shepard felt the power dip and a lurch as the ground came rushing up. The airframe creaked under G-force as Adams drove juice to the rotors. The pitch threw Shepard against his harness again, and he dropped his weapon on its sling and snatched for a handhold. As he secured a grip, the sudden violence of the manoeuvre flung Token across the bench and Mills rushed to haul him back as he slid towards the open door.

"Gauntlet. One-Four. Status."

"We're okay." Stress had crept into Adam's response.

"Ah, we have more vehicles. Small arms. West. Eleven o'clock." The Lynx pilot's voice was collected. A banking right-hand turn offered his crew of SBS troopers range on the approaching hostiles.

Shepard swapped hands, craning his neck as he leaned out the door. Two pickups raced along the low road and climbed the on-ramp.

A whoosh of ignition and the trail of a wild RPG streaked from the ground.

"Crossan!" shouted Shepard. The downdraft of the Lynx whipped the smoke into tight coils.

"I've no shot, Skip."

The detonation obscured the carnage on the carriageway. A billowing ash cloud blew across the road but through the swirl, Shepard caught sight of Kestrel stumbling to her feet, one arm wrapped across her tummy and limping on her right leg. The man who had first joined her crawled from behind the wheel arch of the now burning truck.

Kestrel popped off a half dozen rounds towards the advancing vehicles. Moving around a concrete bollard, she waved up at the chopper.

"They're screwed," said Mills.

"Trident. Gauntlet. Permission to go feet wet."

"Negative Trident. Supporting fire only. Gauntlet dropping from Fox-Nine."

Shepard watched as the vehicles hit the bottleneck and discharged their occupants, the armed group fanning out to approach under cover. Kestrel, going in the opposite direction, was moving too slow.

Crossan and Heath cracked off shots into the cars, receiving bursts of return fire. Another RPG raced into the sky but flew harmlessly between the aircraft.

Haley Adams spooled up the Merlin and swept east across the interchange, a figure of eight turn, crossing beyond where Kestrel was sheltering by the bollards from a fusillade of small arms fire. She wasn't going to make it. He turned to his sergeant.

"Mark, get the rounds down on those RPGs. I want a hundred per cent suppression on those positions."

"Skip."

Shepard looked down as the roadway roared by underneath. The comms net chattered with status updates from Canning and the pilots of the other birds and as Adams banked the Merlin the troops on the ground unleashed a fusillade at the aircraft and another RPG streaked wildly into the sky.

Shepard wrapped a wrist around the grab strap and listened on his SELEX, waiting for one of two things to happen, Canning to receive word from TAC to abort or one of the Jihadis to get lucky and bring down a chopper. Neither of the options was going to pull Kestrel out of the shit she was in or secure the intelligence that would put the Russians back in their box.

He made a decision as the ding of small arms fire hit the Merlin's airframe. Dropping the strap he thumbed his mic.

"Haley?"

"We're okay, it didn't do any damage," she said.

"I'm getting off."

"Negative. We aren't landing in that."

"I'm not asking you to land. Cut us low across the berm."

"Shepard…"

"They aren't going to make it."

As he said the words, he watched as Kestrel stood and waved at the helo, pain and fear etched on her face. Unseen, her companion approached from behind. Raised his AK-47 and took aim at her back.

Shepard snatched up his rifle, aim-point rising and falling as the Merlin rose above the carriageway.

A three-round burst, the first going wide and the second two catching the target centre mass.

Slinging the carbine under his arm, he slapped at the harness restraint as Adams banked the bird through forty-five degrees.

"On my mark.."

Shepard moved to the edge of the airframe. Keyed his SELEX.

"Secondary LS Bronco."

"Roger, Bronco." The airframe shuddered as Haley Adams flared the nose and killed the power. The Merlin froze in place fifty metres downrange of Kestrel.

"Gauntlet. One-Four…"

Shepard didn't hear the rest of Canning's dispatch as he leapt from the aircraft, the sudden wash of rotor draft deafening, and then the hard crunching impact as he hit the ground in a roll.

"One-Four. One-Four. Man overboard."

Mills and Token unleashed suppressing fire from the Merlin's open door as Adams pushed the cyclic. The nose dipped and the aircraft gathered pace then arced up and away from the primary LS.

"One-Four. All call signs, be advised. Blue. Blue. Blue. Friendly on the ground. Neptune is feet wet."

Chapter 12

Feriha pushed her back against the concrete blocking bollard, gunfire cracking around her and the dull roar of aircraft engine and the distinctive whop, whop, whop of rotors overwhelming her senses.

Ambushed.

It made sense now. Whoever had killed Ibrahim hadn't left the corpses to rot, but had somehow lain in wait and tracked them across the city to the pickup point.

The grind of gears and the screech of tyres announced more militia. Feriha flinched as the figure in the helicopter's doorway opened fire.

The grunt from behind told her the shots had hit Reza. She raised her arm against the downdraft as the machine banked and held a brief hover, incredulous as a soldier tumbled from the open doorway and then forlorn as her flight to salvation rose high and away into the sky, gunfire pouring from the open door as the aircraft passed overhead.

She took a glance behind. Reza lay dead. Blood spattered up his face and pooled under his body. Thirty metres away, a black-clad figure rose from cover. He took aim only to be shot in the chest.

Movement. A scramble of boots. Feriha spun and raised Ibrahim's Makarov.

"I'm on your side, miss." Shepard pushed the barrel away.

"Peashooter's not going to help us in this fight, grab the rifle." Shepard propped an elbow on the bollard and fired off single shots. Each found a target.

Above and to the north, the Lynx with Crossan and Heath aboard continued to offer support. Large calibre rounds from the L96s keeping heads down up range of the SBS operator and Christmas Porter's spy.

Feriha scrambled from cover and dragged the AK-47 free of Reza's grasp.

"Your friend just tried to kill you."

"What?"

Shepard fired two three-round bursts. Sporadic, poorly aimed return fire zipped overhead.

"Who was he?"

"A contact. Resistance."

Shepard shook his head. "Two seconds later you'd have been dead."

"No..."

"Is the intel secure?"

"I have it..." Feriha tugged at the rucksack settled at her feet. The soldier hoisted it with one hand and pushed it into her arms.

"We're moving. Are you hit?"

"No. I'm..."

Shepard fired again and then turned. Pushed her against the bollard. A cursory check from head to toe. A nod of satisfaction. Clothes peppered with shrapnel tears but only superficial cuts and grazes.

"On my mark, we track back to those steps, then drop to the underpass and get lost in those alleyways. Fast as you can. Ready?"

"Ready."

Shepard unclipped an M18 grenade from his vest. Pulled

the pin and flicked the lever, then launched it in a high arc.

"All call signs. Neptune. How copy?"

"Gauntlet. Neptune. Solid copy."

"Smoke out. Focused fire on mark. Copy."

There was a hiss of static in his ear. He could imagine Major Canning roaring in angry frustration.

"Copy. Good smoke."

Shepard looked at the Syrian agent. The next moments were vital if they were to slip the noose. She was starting to wobble, caught in an ambush, almost killed by a suicide bomber and then by her own contact. Who could blame her for being on the edge? He placed a firm grip on her shoulder.

"I'm going to get you out of here."

A single nod.

The HH-60 circled overhead, 30mm chain guns spinning up and adding to the suppressing fire already coming from the Lynx and the Merlin.

"Go!"

Chapter 13

Dimitri Yegorov looked at the carnage and spat on the ground.

The overpass stank of battle. Fires still smouldered and smoke drifted on the hot wind sweeping across the flat plains that skirted the main highway. A few bodies still lay where they had fallen, while fifteen more had been dragged into a haphazard square and piled up. Their cache of abandoned weapons stacked alongside as the flies feasted on the open wounds.

Low grunts and groans emanated from the injured, who were propped against the central reservation, bloody, dusty and still in shock that the surprise attack and their overwhelming numbers had been quashed.

Yegorov shook his canteen, unscrewed the cap, and poured some lukewarm liquid into his mouth.

"Soldiers? You people are abysmal. You should be ashamed."

"Colonel, I thought surprise was the better strategy. We had the woman cornered and one soldier fell from the helicopters…"

Yegorov pulled his pistol and shot the militia commander in the face. The shot echoed across the carriageway and the square below.

"Who is in command?"

The groans of the wounded and the dull conversations between smoking men silenced.

"Anybody?"

The rev of a diesel engine broke the silence. A slew of tyres and the ratchet of a handbrake. Angry calls.

"Yegorov. Put your fucking gun away. These men are on your side!" Khalid Al-Salam strode purposefully between the abandoned vehicles and the pile of bodies.

"God help us then." The Russian holstered his Makarov and turned to face the scowling militant.

"What did you think was going to happen when you gassed that village? The Americans were going to wring their hands?"

"It's all they normally do. Their administration had no stomach for a fight with us after Libya and the rest of their coalition only follows because they are told to," Yegorov sneered.

"We'll see how that changes if they get that footage."

"We would already have it but for the incompetence of these fools."

"These fools killed the leader of the Western Wolves…"

"I wanted him alive!" Yegorov exploded. Spittle sprayed from his mouth. "Dead men cannot talk."

"It will disrupt any retaliation while they regroup."

"I don't want them to regroup, I want them destroyed. Wiped out." Yegorov threw his canteen across the carriageway. "Is it not convenient? This Wolf offers up a spy and has his throat cut before he can give more, then, rather than catch the bloody woman these idiots let her escape."

The Russian faced off against the equally imposing Syrian fighter.

"I think there is more than one rotten apple in this barrel, Khalid."

Al-Salam shook his head.

"You assist. You do not presume to direct the objectives of our president. This is not your country."

Yegorov took a step forward.

"Your useless president begged for our help because his army and your bloody militias couldn't unite and turn back a rabble of shopkeepers and washerwomen."

Yegorov spat on one of the dead.

"You couldn't even manage to get this city under control by yourself, could you? It has been my contacts, my intervention, and my weapons that are turning the tide for you now."

"It is not your war," said Al-Salam.

"Don't try and patronise me, Khalid. You think I believe that your hand in this is noble?" Yegorov laughed. "You hold no allegiance to the president or the people. You want to light the fires of jihad and watch the world burn."

"I follow the caliph and we have one common purpose, to see this country and then the next fall under our flag."

"I have my own purpose and set my own objectives, Khalid, and time is wasting. I want this district swept. We've eliminated the problem in Misraa and the last of the rebels harassing the chokepoint between the crescent and Highway five-five are scrambling in what's left of this district. I want them running like rats, and on the way, this soldier and spy need to be captured and whatever film they have destroyed. I'll cut them apart piece by piece after that and once they have told me all they can about the Yankee's operations, you can have whatever is left of your rabble drag them through the streets and see how that plays out on the Western news networks."

The Russian whistled and his men stomped out cigarettes and shouldered weapons.

"I need to move these men back for treatment," said Khalid

Al-Salam at the retreating figure.

Yegorov's stride stuttered to a stop.

He snatched up an abandoned AK-47 from the pile beside the bodies and cocked it. Turned to the barrier of injured men and squeezed the trigger. The burst of gunfire stitched indiscriminately into the mass. When the first clip emptied Yegorov thumbed the release catch and swung the empty magazine forward, releasing it to the ground as he snatched up another, re-cocked and emptied a second and then a third magazine left to right across the scrambling men.

As the last clip clacked empty, he threw the weapon across the ground and pointed at the Syrian.

"Do not test my patience, Khalid. Get anyone who can move into those alleyways and flush out my prey." He jutted his chin at the chain of bleeding bodies.

"If any of this lot are still alive, finish them off and then make your way to the objective."

Chapter 14

"Neptune, how copy?"

Shepard sidestepped a huge water-filled pothole and guided Kestrel by the arm into a side alley running ninety degrees west off the one they were travelling.

The sounds of battle had faded and the whump, whop, whump of rotors had receded, leaving him confident that the team had created enough havoc to facilitate a head start on the hunt that would soon come after them.

His SELEX blipped again.

"Gauntlet, Neptune copy, over."

"Solid copy."

"Status?"

"Kestrel secure. Oscar Mike to secondary LS, Bronco. ETA to be advised. Confirm net?"

He stopped, outstretched an arm to stop Kestrel stepping out into another cross street.

An extended barrage of automatic gunfire echoed across the shattered rooftops.

"Echo Net. Carbon. One. One. Charlie."

"Copy. Carbon. One. One. Charlie." Shepard dialled in the secure channel on the VHF.

"Neptune, be advised hostiles moving in force south of your last known position. Overwatch is requested but unavailable at this time."

"Roger. Moving south-west. Confirm when overwatch is in play. Neptune out."

Shepard listened but only heard the whine of the wind through the ruins of the street and the flapping of bullet-scarred sun awnings, the dusty blue and white cotton stretched between buildings on either side of the narrow passages that offered shade from the sun and cover from the rooftops to the west.

If he had control of the hunting party, he would have men on the lid of the tall apartment building. It had a panoramic view from east to west and, although blind to the low narrow alleys, was the perfect roost to observe the squares and major intersections that he was going to have to negotiate on the way to Bronco.

"Wait. Wait. Just one second," said Feriha.

"Lady, we don't have a second."

"I need to catch my breath?"

"We need to keep moving. There's nowhere near enough concrete between us and that militia to slow down yet."

"Okay. Okay." Feriha huffed out a breath and winced. Felt a sharp jag under her right breast. Pressed three fingers on the area and gasped.

"Let me see?" Shepard paused. The woman flinched as he pulled the tails of her shirt loose and hitched the material up. No blood or visible injuries.

"The pressure wave of the bomb might have broken a rib. We'll look when we find a place to rest. Can you keep up?" he said.

"I'll try."

"What's your name?"

"Feriha. Feriha Najir."

"Feriha, I'm Tom. I promise I'll get you out of here, but we need to move. You're going to have to put up with the pain until I find us a safe spot. Just keep putting one foot in front of the other." He gave what he hoped was a reassuring smile.

"Where are we going? You're taking us the wrong way." Feriha pointed over his shoulder. "We will be boxed in if we go into the city. If we head to the desert, there is a chance we will be collected. Ibrahim's men will come to find him."

"We go into the city. You couldn't outrun an asthmatic mongrel, never mind a bunch of vehicles over open ground."

"I just need a minute," she protested.

Shepard nodded his head, took an impatient glance behind. He gripped her shoulders.

"You can do this. I'll get you and your intel out of here, but you have to do what I say."

Feriha fell back against the wall and rested. Sucking in shallow breaths. They were easier than the gulp of air she needed but still smarted. She looked at the lone soldier, his confidence belying the peril of their situation.

"You are on your own. I was supposed to get out on the helicopter."

"You weren't supposed to almost get us shot down."

"I didn't know..."

"Who was the other fella?"

Feriha shook her head and shrugged as she pushed herself off the wall. Shepard reached out for the rucksack.

"Give that here, I'll carry it. The man you brought to the bridge?" He guided her by the arm across the narrow passage between windowless businesses and the shell-damaged facades of terrace housing.

"Reza Yousef. He's a fixer. A go-between. He distributes medicines and information for me to the Western Wolves."

"He was working with the resistance?"

"Yes. He had secured transport with my contact in the Wolves. When we arrived at the mosque, they were dead."

"I think he played you. Led in the ambush."

"He wouldn't…"

"Look, I saw him about to shoot you and my guess is they made him a better offer." Shepard paused and cleared the junction, sweeping left and right.

"My question is, how much did you tell him?"

"I didn't tell him anything. I was waiting to explain myself once we had secured passage out of the city."

"That's something then."

Shepard needed the woman's local knowledge. He had a destination and a vague direction but she would know the winding streets, short-cuts and, most importantly, the areas to avoid as they raced across the shattered town.

"Where are we going?" Feriha scurried behind the soldier, taking a wary check behind every dozen steps.

"The Mehmet Tal Palace."

"The old hotel?"

"Yep."

"That's miles from here."

"It is. If you can pick up the pace or suggest a way to get there quicker I'm listening."

"You mean like a vehicle?"

"You got one handy?"

"No."

"No. Of course not." Shepard sighted down a broad avenue that they needed to cross. Thankfully, once more all was quiet.

"If you're taking us direct, then once we get to the end of El-Jabal centre we will run into militia. Al-Waleed controls the crescent of parkland surrounding the Mehmet Tal."

"They do."

"You're not worried about them?"

"Not as much as they need to worry about me."

Chapter 15

"Has the son of a bitch got a death wish?" McPeak slammed a palm on the table.

Major Canning had his ballistic helmet tucked under his arm like a football, and Mark Mills to his right remained in full battle dress.

"The LS was hot. Neptune made the call to secure the asset and divert to LS two."

"That wasn't his call to make. Was it, Major?"

"No, sir." Canning's jaw flexed as he ground his molars together.

"That entire area is effectively enemy territory. If I send in the QRF with that hornet's nest stirred up it will escalate into another Battle of Mogadishu." McPeak blew out a frustrated breath and turned to the monitors of the TAC.

"Where is our air asset?"

"On station, way out west. I've requested a re-task but they are bingo fuel. It's a couple of hours turn around, sir."

"We need to offer him something. Are we seriously saying there isn't one drone we can't get into position while we look at options?" Mark Mills took a step forward and Canning raised a placating palm.

"JSFAW can get us back out and on the ground to act as support. We have to do something," Mills implored. Canning shifted his helmet and spoke in a bid to dampen Mills misplaced enthusiasm.

"Colonel, this isn't something new to Neptune. He has been operating behind enemy lines and in that AO specifically. If we…"

"I can't risk the two of them falling into the hands of Dimitri Yegorov, much less put your team on the ground as well, Sergeant," said McPeak. He nodded at Canning. "I know what you're saying, Major. Captain Shepard's reputation precedes him."

Canning looked to his SBS subordinate.

"Mark, tell the boys to get some food down them and rearm. When we get the nod, you'll be going back in, but not until then."

"Aye, aye." Mills dipped his head to both superiors as Canning continued.

"Two bodies with local knowledge have a better chance of making it to LS Bronco without incident than rolling in land, air, and heavy handed to pull them out but we need to consider running some interference…"

"You're right, Major."

The three men turned as Christmas Porter entered the TAC. She had a satphone in her hand and placed it on the desk. McPeak nodded at the equipment.

"Line is dead. I'm assuming Kestrel's was damaged. I know you boys like your toys, but a smash operation will just get bogged down. It's a warren of dead ends and kill zones in there. We're going to have to let them work it out for themselves."

"The skipper has put his arse on the line to pull out your asset, you can't be happy to leave him in there alone?" said Mills.

"Sergeant, he's put the lives of our aircrews, operators, and this base in jeopardy because at some point we are going to have to go in and dig him out of the shit pit he climbed into. He's an idiot."

"And your precious intelligence?" Mills squared off against the woman.

Christmas Porter huffed a laugh at the posturing. She shrugged.

"You win some, you lose some. I won't deny it's important, but I'll tell you this, I'd rather have lost it than have the militia cut off your friend's head for the world to watch."

The room fell silent as Porter's bleak picture settled over them, no one in any doubt what fate awaited Shepard and the asset if Al-Waleed caught up with them or they fell into the clutches of Yegorov.

"Have you any unofficial assistance on the ground we can offer him, Christmas?" said McPeak.

"I've just been on with my locals. She's one of their assets too. Problem is, I've now got a missing, presumed dead, resistance commander and crew. His 2IC is reticent about any follow-up trips after the massacre at Misraa and losing his chief in one day. The information he had from the ground is that Al-Waleed are mopping up following the ambush and cracking down on the population for leads."

McPeak frowned and rubbed his chin.

"Thanks, Christmas. Major, I'm sorry, but it looks like your boy is on his lonesome until we get air over the city and see what we're up against."

McPeak walked up behind the TAC. "Danny, monitor the E&E frequency for updates on Neptune's progress. If he can make it to Bronco in one piece, he better hope we hear him calling for a cab."

Chapter 16

Shepard paused as the eerie silence of the past hour broke with the occasional child's wail or the loud staccato barking of dogs, the sounds of rudimentary civilisation added to by the smells, which were both strong and at extremes.

Wood smoke and gas wafted the aroma of cooking and spitting fats on the air until the stink of ablutions and sewage overpowered them as they passed overflowing and open drainage channels and manhole covers.

"We have to be careful. We can't risk anyone giving away our location to the militia." Shepard watched two small children scramble down a pile of crushed rock and sprint across the street to disappear into the shattered doorway of another property.

"These are poor people."

"All the more reason to keep a low profile."

"We are in no danger here."

"Listen, we're in it up to our necks. I'm not exactly inconspicuous and if you'll forgive me saying so, you look like shit. As soon as we get clocked, we'll be public enemy number one."

"We are not the enemy of these people." Feriha scowled. Those left in the ruins were scratching a feeble existence. Surviving. If they had a side, it was not that of the militias nor the government.

"Not directly, no. But handing us over would make them richer than a rock star."

Shepard held up a hand to halt her progress and took a knee. The render and brickwork of the building he had chosen for cover was in good repair, a section of mural remained pristine and in surreal contrast against the bombed-out neighbouring wrecks.

He peered around the corner.

Across the street, the frontage of every house had been engulfed by piles of uneven brick and twisted mounds of rebar. Roof tiles paved the roadway for fifty metres and, three hundred metres beyond, in a small square amid the toppled balconies and cracked pavements, about fifty people were scattered in tight groups. Dirty, dusty, and quiet as they moved from stall to stall where they had set kiosks up in shattered ground-floor windows or on the dented bonnets of ruined vehicles.

Several men sat kerbside smoking, ages ranging from young to very old. Opposite, a group of young boys filled containers with water from a standpipe and the two children who had scrambled down the rock pile moments earlier appeared from the opening of a dwelling on the edge the area. They ran across the street, boarded the rear door of a broken-down bus and then exited through the front leaping from the top steps and scrambling around the rubble piles, skirting the boys at the standpipe before crashing into the robes of two women who were handling bright red tomatoes at one stall.

"We need a way around this souk. Can you guide us through?"

Feriha shook her head. If they had stayed east or had exited from the 410 south, she would have had a grip on how to negotiate the small pockets of refugees. Here she was unsure.

"If we can backtrack and go east, I might be able to find us a way into the smuggler's tunnels that will bring us up beyond the crescent parkland. But here…" She shrugged.

"We can't go back." Shepard pursed his lips and peered back around the corner. They were relatively well shielded by the rubble and the distractions of the meagre market. If they could cross the open road and enter the buildings opposite, he was confident they could track west and then bear back towards the Mehmet Tal after a kilometre or so.

"Maybe I could ask them for help?"

"Absolutely not. We don't know their affiliations."

"Look at them." Feriha pointed at the gathering. "I'm a doctor. I can offer them some help for some in return."

Shepard didn't like it, but he could see the merit in her suggestion. Several in the crowd sported poorly-fitted slings or bandages. There were head wounds, limb injuries, and poorly-crafted wooden stakes being used as crutches.

"It's too risky."

Shepard settled back into his cover and looked at the agent.

"I'm going first." He gestured a zigzag route across the road. "From here to the van and then to the building across the street. When I signal, you follow the same route. Low and fast don't stop. Okay?"

Feriha nodded.

Shepard checked his kit. Nothing loose. He gripped his carbine and checked one last time. Clear.

"Ready?"

Feriha nodded. She had a bit of colour back in her cheeks. Shepard tapped her on the knee and pushed off the wall.

Immediately clearing the corner, he took a stumbling step to the right and out into the open as a blur of red flashed in his peripheral vision. Pivoting on his left leg, he snapped up his weapon and dropped the sight over the target.

She was about seven years old, her red tracksuit white with dust from the knees down and the elbows up. Her dark eyes were big as saucers and her mouth agape in surprise.

"Hi, little lady." Shepard eased the assault rifle away, kneeling and raising a hand. The child stood transfixed. He glanced at Feriha still in cover and gave a brief shake of his head.

Then the child screamed.

In a flash, the kid had done a one-eighty and was sprinting back towards the crowd, howling at the top of her tiny lungs.

"Move!" Shepard shouted, pointing across the street. He snapped the carbine to shooting position and watched the market.

Feriha broke cover and ran, slipping and stumbling on debris but staying upright as she crossed the street to crouch behind new cover.

The noise was as familiar to Shepard as the bang of dustbin lid on the pavements of West Belfast and had the same purpose. Warning. Incursion. Intruders.

The women of the market snatched their children to their sides and took up their high-pitched trilling ululation.

"Lililililililil…"

He fired once into the air, the shot having the desired effect. Heads dipped and the crowd scattered.

Shepard spun from the road and sprinted after Feriha.

❖

"Up!"

Shepard grabbed at and missed the agent's arm as he leapt over the low wall and barrelled through the opening where the door of the building should have been. Sliding to a stop, he reached out and snatched her to her feet, pulling her into the squalid, semi-dark.

The air was heavy with heat and mildew as he led the way

along a short hallway and turned into a small parlour.

The room was thick with dust that churned up under their feet.

"This way. Quick. Move." Shepard changed tack, exiting back outside through a shattered wall and into a small courtyard.

As Feriha stumbled back into the open air, Shepard pointed at a set of intact steps that led up to flat roofs festooned with bent aerials and bullet holed satellite dishes.

"Speed over security. We go up and we go fast across the rooftops. Stay with me. You see anything, you shout it out." His stern look elicited a sharp nod.

The SBS captain took the steps two at a time, easing his sights above the parapet that fringed the steps and offered a low protective wall around the square roof.

He popped up and took a knee. Sighting west across the roof, he could see the route was immediately clear. At the furthest end, his view was blocked by strings of laundry and dusty mats hanging on cuttings of thin rope that were tied between old television masts and painted flagpoles. To the left, the taller apartment dwellings overlooking the path they would need to take held the greatest concern of opening contact with the locals. To the right, there was the broad gap of the main street below and its suspended sun awnings attached to similar buildings on the other side.

Shepard stood and began to move with fast tactical precision. Weapon up, sighting left along the open windows. Searching for movement. A glance behind. Feriha was close on his heels, palming away a thick coaxial cable loosed from its satellite dish.

Shepard was quick but careful. Debris from strikes on the apartments across the street had spilled across the lower roofs. Webs of cables snaked underfoot and stakes of rusted supporting rods jutted up, seeking to trip the unwary. He paused as he reached the parapet.

It was a short three-foot hop across to the next roof. He reached for the Syrian agent.

"You first. I'll cover."

Feriha nodded and took one step up onto the low wall and sprang across the gap, landing easily on the far side.

Shepard followed and took up point again as they traversed the next rooftop. When they reached the edge, they followed the same routine.

"When we get to the end of the next rooftop, we do down into the alleyway and push west for a few minutes before we find more cover. Are you okay?"

Feriha was breathing heavily and holding her side.

"Is it your ribs?"

"I'm fine. I jarred them when I landed." She waved him on. "I'm fine. I understand. We need to keep going."

Shepard stood aside and let her jump again.

She was heavier on her feet this time. The gap was no greater than the previous few, but she stumbled as she landed. Her right leg slipped wide, traction lost on broken tiling. Feriha threw up a hand to grab at the rope of laundry for support. The pegs popped, and the sheet whipped free as Shepard threw himself across the drop.

He was mid-flight when several of the surrounding sheets tore loose from their moorings. He hit the parapet and rolled left as angry calls rang out. A crash of automatic gunfire. A glimpse of bandolier and the polished wooden stock of Kalashnikov.

Feriha was scrambling to free herself from the shroud of laundry that tangled her limbs.

Shepard pushed himself up, sweeping the carbine to track for targets as more sheets tore free and more voices rang out.

He sensed movement to his right, sight and sound dulled by a heavy woven kilim swaying under the buoyed ropes.

The barrel of an AK-74M clashed against his chin, knocking him onto his backside, and the sound of the weapon's cocking handle preceded the heat of muzzle flash, and then the heavy impacts to his legs.

Chapter 17

The captor was aggressive and his touch heavy handed. The hard iron barrel of the Russian-made assault rifle once again jabbed Shepard in the back as it prodded him down the narrow stone stairwell into the building's basement.

They had overpowered him with ruthless efficiency on the roof. The first glancing blow to his jaw had been followed up with several heavy kicks to his legs, and then a second and a third gunman materialised from between the tangled sheets, brandishing weapons and more threats.

As they dragged Feriha to her feet and disarmed her she was vocal in her protests, continuing her tirade as they marched her down to the street. Shepard's seizure was taken with a little more care but a lot less grace than they afforded the woman. Dragged to his knees, disarmed and disrobed of radio, weapons and the rucksack, his hands were zip-tied before he was hauled up and prodded to follow after Kestrel.

Communication between the men was quiet, controlled, and efficient. They were armed with clean-looking Kalashnikov rifles and dressed in a haphazard collection of civilian clothing and military uniforms. It was hard to distinguish if the men were pro-government militia, allies to the Free Syrian Army and the coalition forces or a shade of grey between. Either way, the situation was going to have to play out. They had been captured and there was little to do but acquiesce, observe, and bide their time.

Shepard's shoulder bumped off the weeping and lime-scaled wall as he ducked under a swaying bare bulb at the foot of the stairway. The light in the space beyond came not from the utilitarian string of electric bulkheads screwed up overhead but from paraffin hurricane lamps and a small opening to the sky. It was a large square space. Aside from the stairwell, an open portal exited at the rear of the room and a smaller crawl space opened to another passage or room where a dull light flickered beyond.

There was no sign of Feriha as he was pushed forward into a shaft of sunlight which pooled on dusty rugs and a collection of cushions supporting half a dozen grim-faced men in muted conversation. Spread out before them, were Shepard's weapon and equipment and Kestrel's pack emptied of its contents of satphone, laptop, camera and memory cards. Shepard's bullish guard stopped him with a tug on his collar and then nudged him to his knees.

The conversation paused, and the faces peered up. A middle-aged, bearded man spoke sharply to the rest. His words tamped down by a slicing gesture from a younger man to his left.

"You are military?"

Shepard dipped his head once. The man's English was refined and far superior to his own capabilities in Arabic.

"You don't look Russian."

"I'm not."

A purse of the lips and a cock of the head. A harsh whisper from the agitated man to the right as they traded words.

"I think this is a misunderstanding, sir."

"Do you? My compatriot here doesn't think so."

Shepard shrugged apologetically.

"He would like to know why you would shoot at families

in the souk."

"I didn't."

"Liar!" The bearded man rose, only to be pushed back down by the younger man.

"I would be very careful how you answer these next questions."

Shepard nodded, aware of his guard's weapon hovering at his back. He could smell the stale cigarette smoke of the man's breath.

"You shot at the souk."

"I had no intention of harming anyone."

"So why shoot?"

"I needed to create a diversion. I have someplace to be."

"It must be important?"

"I'm on a timetable. So, if you might help me on my way. I'm sure you would be well rewarded."

The man scoffed a laugh.

"You think I need more dollars?"

Shepard looked around the room.

"I'd say every penny counts."

"You people think you can just throw dollars at a problem and solve it. You do not understand. What good is money to me? To these men? Our people? Where do we keep it? Where do we spend it? Look around you, soldier."

"Sir. With respect. I offer compensation for the trouble I've caused and for the safe passage of myself and my colleague."

"The woman?"

"Yes."

"Why are you travelling with one of our women?"

"I'm escorting her."

"Where?"

"To a place of safety."

"Is this not a safe place?" He gestured around the room. The group's weapons were stacked against the walls. Thick concrete protected them from the street and there were guards.

"Maybe for you, sir. It doesn't feel too safe for me."

An elderly man to the speaker's right moved, his face a grimace as he shifted positions and spoke.

"What is this?" He pointed to Kestrel's possessions.

"Media equipment."

"Media." He nodded. His own accent was thick but his English still passable. "Highlighting our plight to the world?"

"I guess so."

"Do you think the world cares about what happens here, soldier?"

"I think so. Governments have put men like me here to help."

"Help? What help have your bombs and guns brought? I know what you are. You are one of the killers in the night. Now you might come for those aligned with the president and the Russians but how long before you come for men like us?"

"I'm not a policymaker, sir. I follow orders."

"Your orders have landed you in a predicament."

"I've been asked to take the lady to safety. To return this equipment. I just seek passage through your territory."

The elder man barked a call and there was a rustle and commotion from the door to the rear.

Shepard stiffened as another pair of guards dragged Kestrel into the room and dumped her on the floor. She shot a glance at Shepard and then at the men. Her eyes widened.

"Doctor, it's been some time."

"Mullah?"

"My grandson raves about his visits to your clinic. I believe you may have inspired him to follow in your footsteps." The elder man held Feriha's gaze.

"Mullah…" Her words faltered. He shook his head. Spared

her the task.

"We found his body with the Irishwoman."

"I'm sorry."

"It is God's will."

The elder put out an arm and the younger man helped him to his feet in a series of jerky arthritic movements. He placed his hand on the doctor's shoulder.

"Jabir had warned them not to go, but my daughter insisted. Who am I to put the concerns of my son above the needs of my granddaughter?" He looked at Shepard. The younger man looked pained, and Shepard realised it was frustration. Impotence at being unable to protect his kin.

"I'm sorry for your loss, sir."

"We are used to loss here, soldier. It has become our way of life. Some see it as God's punishment but I see it as his blessing. My family is with him now. My resolve to see my country free is purified with every passing. It is my sworn duty, not the duty of foreigners."

Shepard conceded the man's belief with a nod.

"Mullah…"

"Are you with this man willingly, Feriha?" said Jabir.

The doctor looked from the mullah to his son. Jabir Habib stared at her stony eyed. She knew the man's reputation; patriotic, fierce, and uncompromising. Habib had been unwilling to abandon the city and the enclave of people left within to join the Wolves in their campaign against the advancing forces of the Russians and their southern militia. Instead he and his men moved position within the city nightly, striking out across the shifting frontline of seized streets and districts. Their increasing guerrilla tactics which initially shocked the opposition's advance had more recently incurred severe and indiscriminate reprisals. It didn't take a tremendous leap of deduction to realise the attack on Misraa was one such attempt to stall the Syrians' campaign of violence and turn his own people against him.

"Mullah, the Irishwoman filmed what happened this morning. If this man can see it into the hands of his superiors, it will go to stalling the Russian aid. Maybe even force their withdrawal."

"Who exactly is this man?" The bearded dissenter spoke up, receiving a sharp retort from Jabir Habib.

"He is Allied Special Forces." Feriha looked to Shepard. There was no point in denying it.

"Captain Shepard."

"You are SAS?" said Jabir.

"Navy."

"We are a long way from the sea, Captain," said Mullah Habib with a knowing nod.

Shepard smiled. The Royal Navy's elite band of brothers had avoided the level of celebrity their compatriots in the Special Air Service had been bestowed, whilst quietly carving a fearsome reputation in combat in the mountains and cities of Iraq and Afghanistan and in battling the scourge of piracy in the Arabian Sea.

"What makes you think you can trust him?" Mullah Habib looked to the doctor.

"He risked his own life to save mine."

"You're sure?"

"I am."

Mullah Habib moved to look Shepard up and down.

"Our men found Ibrahim," he said.

"Reza Yousef called him to get me out," said Feriha.

"The Wolf had his throat cut. Like a dog."

Feriha looked to the ground, a shroud of guilt washing over her.

"You are a healer, Feriha. How have you ended up in the midst of all this death?"

"I'm a daughter of Syria."

"You are, with a right to fight, but how can you align yourself with the occupiers and not your brothers?"

"They offer us help. Arms. Medicine. Sanctuary. We will get our country back, but hiding in the rubble and striking like thieves is not the way. Your supply lines are stretched. You have no food. How long before the only way to fight back is by throwing stones?"

The old mullah laughed.

"You might have a point."

"Her man led the Russians to the highway where we hoped to extract, sir. We were ambushed and had to abort. I was put on the ground to get the doctor and her evidence to the Mehmet Tal," said Shepard. "Diplomatically that footage can force a Russian withdrawal, at least temporarily. Practically, if you work with us, we can have military advisers and equipment in place during the stand-down which will put you in a better position to launch a counteroffensive."

Habib nodded. Jabir looked unimpressed.

"You cannot cross to the Tal without passing through the crescent parkland, and it is heavily occupied."

"I hoped to guide us through the smugglers' tunnels," said Feriha.

Habib shook his head and looked to his son.

"You cannot use the tunnels."

"Why? We have to get this to the coalition. When Russia's hand in the massacre is exposed, the West will act."

"They have not acted yet."

"There is a bigger picture, sir."

"Not to us." Mullah Habib sighed. "Your leaders and your people are not oblivious to this conflict, yet they have chosen to fight in the shadows. I would not wish what has happened here on anyone else, but there comes a time when one must act oneself."

"Airing the destruction of that village could be the catalyst."

"I shall not trade one occupying force for another." Habib looked Shepard in the eye, appraising the younger man. The eyes were hooded, wiry lashes narrowed, as he assessed the soldier's capabilities.

"Foreign powers using my country to bloody each other's noses on the world stage must end. We agree on that. Yes?"

Shepard and Feriha nodded in unison.

"Your accent? Scottish?"

"Northern Irish."

"You know something of conflict then?"

"Some." Shepard offered a tight smile. He had grown up in the middle of bitter sectarian division. An observer of death and destruction. Tainted by his own grief. The tragic loss of family. Of a wife and a child. He could empathise with the Syrian. But for the grace of God, his country could have been a reflection of this one.

"Are you a student of history?"

"I passed my exams."

"If I spoke of Operation Fortitude?"

Shepard nodded.

"A deception against the Germans in advance of D-Day."

Mullah Habib clicked his fingers. A glint in his eye.

"Exactly." He nodded to the guard. The man slung his AK-74 and Shepard was jostled as the man pulled his arms up. The sudden snap as he slashed the zip ties free.

"Thank you." He massaged life back into his wrists and fingertips.

There were murmurs from the rest of the men in the room but these were silenced when Jabir spoke.

"My father is a student of warfare. My friends here believe we should put all we have into a final assault."

"The Charge of the Light Brigade." Habib closed his eyes

wistfully.

The romantic image of Cardigan's cavalry charge against the Russian guns at Balaklava in painting and on screen came to Shepard's mind. It hadn't ended well for them and he suspected a similar action by the ragtag militants around him would end in similar disaster.

"Al-Waleed and the Russians are entrenched in the crescent parkland, which bisects the city. Their forces have control as far west as the Grand Bazaar and as far east as the river. Whoever holds the crescent holds control," said Mullah Habib.

"We have plans to relieve them of their stranglehold."

"We have to get to the Mehmet Tal and get that film out, Mullah. Please. We need your help." Feriha put her palms together.

Habib looked to his son and gave a curt nod. Jabir spoke sharply to the guards and several left, Shepard's guard retiring to the back of the room beside the stairway, a wary eye remaining on the SBS captain. The group of men rose from their cushions.

"We can help you."

"Thank you..." Feriha reached out to take the mullah's hands.

Jabir picked up Shepard's Colt carbine and passed it back.

"We can help you," repeated Jabir. "But in order to help you. You must help us fight."

Chapter 18

It wasn't the worst plan Shepard had ever seen. That being said, it wasn't the best either, not by a long shot.

"The ground to the right is protected by the watchtowers and fortified barriers while the left takes advantage of the crescent's geography." Jabir guided a fingertip along the horizon from their position inside a top-floor flat in a block of four high-rises that overlooked the low ruins of bombed-out thoroughfares and once-teeming shopping streets.

Shepard passed the binoculars right to left as the militant laid out his plan again, settling the optics on one of the militia barriers. The defenders had narrowed the approach by bulldozing rubble to form a narrow chokepoint which could be fired upon from three sides while limiting the attackers' perspective to targets ahead. On clearing this channel, heavy concrete cubes and concertina wire had been laid to blockade the roads into the parkland and beyond. Each position was manned on the ground and by a rotating guard in what they called a watchtower but which was just a wooden platform on stilts.

Behind this initial line of defence lay a fallback trench and then another set of anti-vehicle countermeasures. Rusted metal I-beams salvaged from the ruins were studded in the ground, a deterrent for the explosive-packed cars and trucks that the militias had tried to use to breach the perimeter and gain a foothold on the inside of the crescent to establish a beachhead from which to launch an offensive.

The defenders also held the advantage of high ground where, on a central plateau overlooking the shallow ridge from the parkland, Hesco barriers protected command and communication structures, accommodation, and ordnance stores. Several of the buildings comprised hastily-erected blockwork, while the majority were converted shipping containers set to task.

Large wire and mesh Hesco bags had been arranged in line and stacked two high with firing ports at equidistant corners on similar flat wooden platforms to the towers.

"It will be a tough scrap, Jabir. You sure you have enough men?"

"You doubt our ferocity?"

"Not at all. I'm concerned that given they have an elevated position and how broad the front is, the potential to be outflanked and outgunned makes your frontal assault little more than a suicide mission."

"Which is why my father speaks of fortitude."

Shepard passed across the binoculars.

"A diversion?"

The militant nodded and beckoned Shepard away from his vantage point to a table of schematics and photographs.

"Just as we are cut off from resupply and free movement, so are the defenders, by your own operations or those of the Western Wolves and my own men. Today, like every month, they receive a significant replenishment of food, ammunition and a rotation of fresh troops."

He highlighted an area on the south side of the crescent where the main trunk road from the city bypass entered the outskirts of the crescent.

"One of our raiding parties against Al-Waleed interests

was captured and executed a few weeks ago. But not before they detailed our plans to attack the resupply today."

"You let men die to plant a lie?"

"They were volunteers to a greater cause, Captain." Jabir shrugged. "Since then we have made sure that the intelligence was corroborated by double agents and our observations and preparations for the attack were subject to scrutiny that would not normally be accepted."

"You plan to draw the defenders away from the base?"

"Yes. When the assault begins, we expect a significant counter-strike. When that happens, we simultaneously launch the real assault and then a convoy against the primary means of access. Here and here." Jabir slid the map across and placed two bullets on the objectives. "We expect the encampment to be lightly defended as all eyes are on the southern assault. God willing, at least one vehicle will succeed in breaching the perimeter pulling what defence remains to repel the third wave." He drew a finger between each of the bulldozed approaches.

"Fifty men. RPGs. Heavy machine guns. It should be enough to hold Al-Waleed and any remaining Russians in contact."

Shepard let out a slow breath. A lot was riding on it running perfectly, and he knew operations seldom went without a hitch. The expected counter-ambush being sprung too early or spotted, one vehicle breaking down on the narrow approach blocking the breaching party, more defenders than anticipated. He cocked his head, weighing the possibilities.

"If the advance teams can set up this scenario, then the assault team might have a chance."

Jabir smiled and nodded enthusiastically at Shepard's lukewarm approval.

"Our teams will use the smugglers' tunnels to enter inside

the cordon and trap the enemy between our forces. It is a formality from there."

"It's rarely a formality, Jabir," warned Shepard.

"Okay, I understand. It is not perfect, but it is the plan. Unless you can get us some air power to bomb the shit out of them first." The Syrian's face held a warm open smile and Shepard couldn't help but return it. The militia and their Russian support had put these people through hell. Who was he to begrudge them the means to take the battle to their oppressors? He nodded.

"I can't promise anything, but I'll see what I can do."

Chapter 19

"Whatever happens you stick by my side and you keep your head down. Okay?"

Feriha fidgeted with her webbing straps. It was the fifth time in as many minutes she had slipped the adjustable tri-bar buckle to ease the fit.

"You don't have to come, you know," said Shepard

Feriha stopped what she was doing and looked up at him.

"You think you have more of a right to this fight than me?"

"No, but between you and me this has been worked out on the back of a box of Camels."

Feriha laughed, dispelling the tension in her face.

"Which is why I am coming."

"Well. Every pair of hands will count and at least I can be sure you won't shoot me in the back. Here." Shepard reached out and pulled her closer. Sliding the buckle and tightening the strap. He gave the spare magazine pouches a tug. All secure.

"Better?"

"Yes."

"How's your ribs?"

"Not as bad."

"Okay. We'll get through this and get you out of here, I promise," said Shepard, offering a reassuring smile.

Feriha reached out and pulled him closer. Planting a kiss on his lips.

"Whoa." Shepard eased the woman back on her heels. "What was that?"

"Thank you." Her expression had calmed and her eyes held steely resolve at the prospect of what was ahead. "Thank you for not abandoning me. For getting us this far."

"I'd hold off on the gratitude until I get us out of this turkey shoot, Doc." Shepard tipped her chin up.

"This might not go how Jabir expects it, so at the first sign of trouble, you get back in those tunnels and you get to the roof of the Tal."

"And you?"

"I'll be right behind you."

They looked at each other. Alone amid the chaos of preparation. Bound by circumstance and duty.

Shepard felt a pang of melancholy crash over him. Guilt for those he had not been able to save. For being two thousand miles away when he should have been at home.

"What's this?"

Feriha reached into his collar and tugged at a chain of polished beads. The rosary slid from below his BDUs. A small silver cross swayed on the end.

"A righteous warrior," she said with a playful edge to her voice.

"Lucky charm. I lost my rabbit's foot." Shepard plucked the cross free and tucked the beads and the memories that went with it back inside his shirt.

He picked up his carbine and four of the fragmentation grenades Jabir had set to the side.

"Let's go watch the fireworks."

Chapter 20

If there was a hierarchy, then Shepard and Feriha were at the bottom of it.

Cresting the heights were Jabir and Mullah Habib and their commanders, including the stern, bearded man who would lead the third wave of infantry, Qusay Mohammed. Each held a set of binoculars which occasionally passed back and forth to subordinate fighters. Shepard didn't need the enhancement to see what was happening far to the south.

A convoy of covered trucks was moving through the dying light of the afternoon, hampered by the ramshackle roads and collapsed buildings as they threaded from the highway to the edge of the city.

The mutterings of the gathered militants intensified and Shepard pulled Feriha aside to get a better view from the edge of the balcony that overlooked the lay-up point.

The trucks were slowing, negotiating the hazards and, Shepard noticed, rather than the high-speed nose to tail train through contested territory that he would expect, the vehicles had spread out.

The short-wave radio hummed. A voice crackled and Jabir returned the call with a short sentence of confirmation, eyes glued to the binoculars and looking at the distant trap.

The flash illuminated the white facades of the derelicts two seconds before the deep boom and plume of dirt and rock launched the first truck into the air, the vehicle flipping twice over before crashing to the ground in flames. A cheer rippled through the gathered ranks at the successful IED explosion and Shepard winced, his eyes darting down to the streets and the hundreds of empty windows that faced the observation point. If they kept up the raucous celebrations, they might as well paint a bullseye on the side of the building while they were at it.

"Allahu Akbar." Mullah Habib raised his hands. Jabir turned and spoke to his gathered commanders.

"This is our day. See your men to their positions." The room emptied on the militant's orders, Qusay Mohammed offering a nod as he passed the SBS captain. Allowing the troops of the second and third wave to melt away into the streets, Shepard then picked up a pair of binoculars and trained them on the defences of the crescent. All eyes in the nearest two watchtowers had turned to face the pop and crackle of ammunition burning off in the hulk of the wrecked truck. A second later there was another flash and low rumbling explosion.

The rest of the convoy peeled left and right, offering themselves broadside to the road ahead. Scrambling from the rubble and the dark entrances to the buildings, Jabir's militants rushed from cover and the bark and crack of weapons rang out as Jabir's not so secret ambush launched.

The rear trucks divested their load of troops and they fanned out, their loose skirmish line afforded cover by the surrounding destruction.

An RPG soared out from the attackers, fishtailing wildly as it rocketed high above the heads of the Russians.

The covered sides of the second and third trucks dropped and mounted DShK heavy machine guns ripped rounds down on the ambush, their deep guttural bark echoing across the distance.

The skirmish line pushed forward, aided by the suppression of the machine guns which had reduced the initial ambush to sporadic potshots.

Exiting the treeline ahead of the trucks and flanking the ambush site, Shepard picked out two heavy BTR-80 armoured personnel carriers as they raced across open parkland, mud and divots thrown up in their wake, top-mounted gunners zeroing the kill zone which had now been turned against the attackers.

Jabir clutched the mic of the short-wave radio in his hand. Placed it to his lips to speak and then waited.

As BTRs crashed from the parkland onto the streets, the streak of a shoulder-mounted rocket launcher slewed across the space and slammed into the cover of the ambush party, its impact explosion throwing rock, debris, and body parts into the air.

Jabir turned to Shepard and smiled.

"It is time."

The militant commander spoke into the short-range mic.

Shepard felt the dull resonance in his chest as the booms and Jabir's tactics played out, the jaws of his second assault snapping closed.

Shepard knew the weapon as the Mark 15 mortar. Colloquially it was called the 'Barrack Buster' and Jabir's comprised six commercial gas cylinders which had been modified to form 320mm mortar tubes, each of the six tubes having been dug in and hidden from the enemy's view with their ordnance of 80kg HE shells fashioned from metre long propane cylinders packed with home-made explosives and shrapnel.

The rapid detonations gave the advancing counterstrike no quarter, and the shells had the effectiveness of flying car bombs. As the first obliterated the two truck-mounted machine guns in a tide of flame and a mushroom plume of black smoke, the next two detonations buried the advancing skirmish line, high-explosive shells striking the buildings that had offered cover but now tumbled tons of block and rubble on top of the panicked men.

Shepard sighted the fourth and fifth as they hit the first APC to lift it clear of its wheelbase, tearing the passenger hold from the cab in a shower of shredded metal and flame. The second APC narrowly avoided the same fate, bouncing over the wreckage of the first and sliding sideways onto the roadway. Its rear doors were exposed to an RPG which streaked from the ambush and slammed home with a dull tinny boom, popping the top cover hatch and sending burning bodies scrambling from the interior.

Jabir barked into the mic.

Kalashnikovs fired into the air in celebration as a second wave of militants flocked from their hidden positions and sprinted towards the parkland. Spotlights and sirens blared from the base, the ambush drawing the defenders to repel the attack on their now exposed southern flank.

"It's working," said Feriha.

Jabir embraced his father then turned to Shepard and Feriha.

"Now we strike the mortal blow."

Chapter 21

Feriha screamed as large clods of earth fell from the tunnel ceiling.

Shepard put out a hand to steady himself. Air support having been denied, he was left to endure the ground trembling underfoot as above them another dull crump of a vehicle-borne IED crashed into the front access gates of the pro-government-held base.

Jabir's sappers had done a good job. The tunnel was low, but not so much that they had to crawl, so the assault team moved quickly over the wooden duct-boards in a stooped crouch. Each of the party had a neon plastic Cyalume strung around their neck while others had been stabbed into the earthen sides or hung from supporting beams to light the way in a ghostly green glow.

"Move. Move. Move." The man behind Feriha coaxed her onwards. Shepard looked back and caught her expression, anxious yet resolute in the eerie light.

The tunnel pressed in on them and although claustrophobia wasn't a particular fear he held, the hastily constructed tunnel buried underneath an orchestrated car bomb assault was an unsettling means of incursion into enemy territory.

Shepard moved again. His carbine carried no torch, but he

had no problems following the man in front through the gloom by the light of the neon markers.

The low crack of individual shots and sustained bursts of automatic gunfire were muffled as Qusay Mohammed's forces pressed forward above their heads, his men rushing into the void created by the first wave of IEDs.

All too suddenly the bodies ahead stacked up, their whispers filtering back down the line. Shepard paused two feet behind the man in front, who turned and passed the message. "Take your light off."

Shepard watched as each necklace light dropped to the floor. His own followed as he turned to Feriha, who was panting.

"Remember to stay with me. Okay?"

She nodded then swallowed as another explosion rocked the tunnel.

A ripple of pressure and wave of sound rolled down the passageway towards them and the bodies surged forward.

A roar of voices and the growing noise of gun battle intensified as Shepard pushed ahead. The tunnel widened to a small circular alcove where three ladders rose at twelve, three and nine o'clock.

Jabir's men had already broken through and were streaming out into the open ground above.

Grabbing Feriha, Shepard ushered her to the front ascent.

"Right behind me."

She nodded, eyes on the patch of sky overhead.

Gunfire erupted above, the fusillade amplified inside the tunnel.

Feriha shouted a warning as Shepard caught movement and shouldered her left as a fighter tumbled back down into the exit hatch. He was dead, the body caught on the rungs, and a clean headshot leaving a burn mark in the centre of his face and a larger gory mess where the back of his skull should have been.

Bellows came from behind as the assault backed up.

"Help me." Said Shepard, stepping up and securing his feet on the rungs, tugging at the man's waistband as Feriha grabbed the arms and hauled. The body jerked free and tumbled in an unsightly heap to the foot of the ladder.

Shepard moved quickly to ascend, his boots slipping on the bloody woodwork. His head and shoulders grazed the hatch.

Dirt and stone sparked around him as he came under fire, the telltale flash of the weapon fifty yards ahead under cover of a low concrete barrier with more muzzle flare erupting along the obstacle in support of the first.

The first dozen of Jabir's militants were laid low, returning fire at the barricade or unloading weapons back down the slopes into the back of the positions Qusay's team were engaging. Another burst of incoming rattled along the lip of the hatch, forcing Shepard to take cover.

Mud and flinty pebbles peppered his helmet as he sheltered and reached to unclasp one of his fragmentation grenades. He pulled the pin and exited cover long enough to lob the explosive across the gap and into the enemy position.

Panicked voices and a warning preceded the dull whump.

Shepard scrambled out of the tunnel and raised his weapon. Moving with practised precision, picking targets and firing single shots, he zigzagged across the space and leapt over the barrier.

Among the dead, one militiaman lay injured but brought his weapon to bear.

Shepard fired two quick shots, striking centre mass.

His new position offered unrestricted sight along the defence barricade and as two more of the enemy ran around the corner to suppress the assault, they strayed into his sights. A rapid burst and they fell. A heartbeat later, Feriha scrambled over the concrete lip, followed by two more militants.

Below at the gate, volleys of undisciplined fire targeted the slopes which had the benefit of suppressing the defenders and allowed the assault team, who were now clearing the tunnels and taking cover, the opportunity to pick them off from their superior position.

Shepard looked right to the first of the objectives Jabir had set.

Designated Watchtower One, the guards had their weapons trained on the assault to the south and had missed the initial surprise attack under their feet. Sweeping around the machine gun nest, the roadway ascended uphill to the plateau and the compound beyond that needed to be secured.

The tower crew were regrouping.

Small arms fire rained down on the attackers, pinning them in cover as the heavy DShK was repositioned.

Shepard unclipped a second frag and lobbed it up and over the guard rail.

The bang was instantaneous as it fell from sight. Screams and a body fell through the hatch.

Rushing for the ladder, he ascended the steps two at a time into the acrid smell of explosives and burned flesh.

Clearing right, he settled his sights on a guard slumped against the wooden rail, his bloody hands holding his gut, intestines lacerated by grenade shrapnel. Shepard fired once.

"Clear above."

He dropped back to the defence line as Qusay broke through on the slopes below and began his advance up the hill. The intensity of the firefight had muted somewhat. Potshots and occasional bursts rang out, but it seemed they had secured the initial ground.

"Captain?"

Jabir moved along the barricade, an arm aloft as Qusay

and his men threaded their way through the I-beams to rally under the watchtower. Jabir's expression was tense but set firm.

"We split right and left. Captain, your objective is to ensure we take the armoury out of commission. If we remove ammunition stores, we remove their ability to fight back. Qusay, you silence them. Target the command and communications hut."

A series of dull booming explosions resounded from the lower slopes as another set of Mark 15 mortars launched, arcing over their heads to land amidst the defenders now hunkered on the plateau.

Rifle fire and cheering loosed into the air as the high explosive ordnance landed along the ridgeline and demolished a section of Hesco block.

"Victory, Captain."

Shepard took the offered hand and then reloaded, pushing the sentiment to the back of his head.

As things stood, the assault was panning out better than he had hoped, but victory for Jabir remained a long way off. They still had two hundred metres of roadway with no cover and an elevated and motivated defence to negotiate before they could set about securing the objectives that would allow the ultimate celebration. Beyond that, he still needed the militant commander to follow through with his promise and get them to the Mehmet Tal for extraction through a fleeing and wounded enemy. From that point of view, the fight to get Kestrel and her incendiary evidence of war crimes to safety was very much a battle in progress.

Chapter 22

The jangle of ammunition pouches and the beat of boots set a rhythm as they moved swiftly along the left-hand roadway to the overshadowing plateau.

Sporadic gunfire still sounded to the south where the pitched battle at the ambush site was dying out in favour of the attackers. Flank secure, the militants would be moving to assault the southern edge of the base compound.

Shepard took a knee and Feriha dropped beside him. The men behind leapfrogged forward thirty yards before dropping and then Shepard rose in turn, and the section assigned to him mirrored the movement.

They crossed the first eight hundred metres without incident until the popping whoosh of a flare launched, the contrail streaming into the sky before it deployed to hang suspended on a small parachute. The brilliant light illuminated the slopes and the rapidly advancing raiding party.

Almost instantly shots began to ring out. Focused single rounds.

The first man went down in seconds. Wounded. The second casualty wasn't so lucky.

"Suppressing fire!" Shepard called out, kneeling and unloading at the muzzle flash above on the ridge.

Around him, weapons began firing, Feriha's AKM chattering on full auto as she emptied a clip.

"Moving!"

Shepard trusted his men to follow as he sprinted ahead to gain ground while behind, the second section took up the fusillade of covering fire. As he slid to his knee, the man beside him gave a low guttural grunt, propelled onto his back as he took a round in the chest.

Shepard swept the carbine up, left hand on the foregrip, stock tight in his shoulder. He dropped the ACOG sight over the shooter as the man's weapon moved to a new target.

A short bark of two rounds and his target dropped; another two at the replacement who popped up to return fire.

Two dead in two seconds. Shepard continued to push forward, Feriha firing from the hip as she ran alongside. He popped the pin on another grenade and lobbed it high into the defensive cover.

Screams split the air after the dull crump of the explosion. Sprinting the last ten metres, he slid to the protection of the Hesco barrier, sighted around the edge, and squeezed off the rest of his clip.

The three Russians took the scything arc of fire point blank. Shepard, ducking back into the cover afforded by the wire mesh and rock wall, reloaded, grateful surprise had fallen in his favour this time.

The armoury had been identified from long-range photographs as a large hangar-style structure of light grey block walls and a curved corrugated roof. It extended back from the roadway opposite the tented mess and accommodation facilities.

The men assigned to the assault surged across the last yards of the rise and formed up around his position.

"Flank right and left. Watch your arcs and keep an eye out for defensive positions. We don't have the sightlines now we're hitting the camp."

Heads bobbed in acknowledgement.

The whoosh of an RPG signalled Jabir and Qusay had made the plateau, the rocket-propelled grenade slamming into a sandbag bunker with a booming crescendo of noise.

The defenders stationed in the block buildings and covering the higher sections of Hesco began to return fire, although it was sporadic under the withering assault by the militants.

"Let's get this over with. Ready? Go! Go! Go!"

Shepard moved the men forward with a short chopping wave.

The two sections split to advance across the ground in front of the mess tents until they could use the cover of the buildings.

Shepard glanced to Feriha, who knelt by his side, concentrating as she covered the immediate area down the iron sights of her AKM assault rifle. Shepard touched her shoulder.

"After three. On the heels of section two. Ready?"

The chug of heavy machine guns roared close by.

Large calibre rounds stitched across the ground, gouts of dirt exploding under the impact, and the bulk of the second section fell under the gunfire.

Shepard hauled Feriha behind cover as a second salvo of the big guns ripped from the right and obliterated the leading ranks of the first assault section, bullets shattering into the protective blocks above his head and the earth in front of his feet. His ears rang, the unexpected noise and the shrapnel of exploding rounds disorientating for a second.

The cannons had an overlapping field of fire. To his right he heard the pop and whoosh of a shoulder-mounted AT4, then the boom as it struck just ahead of Jabir's advance. A wave of gravel and rubble washed over the militants.

"It's a trap."

The cargo coverings of the mess tents whipped loose as they were cut down. Nose to tail in a cavalry square, eight technicals had been deployed in two tight formations, their firepower overwhelming against the infantry.

As the technicals poured hundreds of rounds at the now frenetic withdrawal, Shepard saw a Russian BTR-80 roar from the cover of the armoury building and track its top-mounted . 50-cal cannon to bear down on him and Feriha.

Chapter 23

Dimitri Yegorov gripped the handles of the .50-cal and yelled as he indiscriminately unloaded the heavy-bore weapon at the attackers. The big APC bucked as it ramped over the edge of the smoother tarmac that floored the plateau and up onto the wide gravel rim that extended from the Hesco perimeter to the compound buildings.

He swept the weapon left as a group of three militants rose from the dirt and sprinted forward for cover. The thunderous report of the weapon vibrated from his fingers on the trigger through his entire body, tracer and heavy rounds killing the three men as his aim cut across their advance.

The wheels of the BTR slewed in the gravel as the driver turned the vehicle to race across the gap between the armoury and the first exposed entrance arch. Its 450hp turbo diesel engine roared as it once again crested an incline and slammed back onto harder tarmac. Yegorov's barrage stitched wide of his target but drove the men to the ground as the shells exploded through the slim cover of shipping crates and wooden supply boxes.

The deception was complete. Cross and double-cross. The Arab militia caught in the web of their own confidence.

The plan to assault the resupply column had been exposed quickly by Khalid Al-Salam. Too quickly for Yegorov's cynical levels of distrust of the militant terrorists to fall for it. It made little sense either. A surprise attack on the column may be successful, even with support coming from the crescent base, but if it was, it would only mean the next time the column would be more heavily defended and the perimeter of the base would be pushed further out into the shattered streets resulting in more territorial losses for the mujahideen.

The true plan had been revealed once Yegorov had become involved. Everyone talks eventually and he was adept at drawing out the truth of those who found themselves enduring his interrogations. In the end, the misery of the men had come too quickly; the Russian relished in their suffering and the early deaths had spoiled his gratification.

The wrinkle of the spy and her escape had been a problem, but the killing of the leader of the Western Wolves, while disappointing made up for that. Now he would crush what resistance remained. This was the final battle. He had drawn in the flies and now, as he wound his web around them, he would put them out of their misery once and for all.

Chapter 24

Shepard dropped the red dot of the aim-point on the head of the technical gunner to the far right and, leaning into the shot, squeezed the trigger. The muzzle jumped skywards, dropping back in time to see a red mist cloud from the back of the man's head.

The chugging dat-dat-dat-dat of one gun was silenced.

Tracking low, he squeezed off another round with the same effect as a second man tried to take control of the weapon.

From the armoury, a steady line of militia were moving to support the technicals who were breaking formation following the devastating surprise attack.

He lined up on the nearest vehicle as it sped away, his first shot sparking off the door column, the second spattering the blood of the driver against the windshield. The jeep slewed wildly left crashing with its neighbour.

Shepard centred the red dot back on the gunner and loosed a triple volley, the impacts sending the man spiralling out of the vehicle and under the wheels of another.

"Move. We need to fall back and regroup with Jabir."

Feriha was firing clip after clip at the infantry moving through the ground between the armoury and their cover in the mouth of the Hesco trench.

"Feriha!" Shepard slapped her on the shoulder as the AKM

clacked empty.

"Go!" He pointed back along the paved path between the two stacks of protective blocks.

She slapped a new magazine home and spun from her knee into a low loping run.

Gunfire zipped over their heads.

Shepard began selecting targets as the remnants of the second section scrambled under fire to the cover of the block barriers, years of practised discipline and experience taking over as he set a relaxed, methodical pace. Target. Fire. Retarget. Fire. Counting out the expelled cartridges as he pulled the trigger.

"Captain?" Shepard loosed the last three rounds in a burst and dropped the mag, turning to jog back towards where Jabir crouched with Feriha, Qusay, and a group of thirteen militants.

"What happened, Jabir?"

"We have been betrayed, but the fight is not lost!"

"You think?" Shepard fired off a salvo of rounds as figures weaved between the cover of the crates in the near distance.

"Get some of these men up on that barrier." He pulled the nearest man to his feet and pushed him towards a step, up onto the Hesco.

"Qusay, tell them to pick their targets. The vehicles can't get down here, but we're going to find ourselves cut off real fast if that infantry is allowed to get in behind us."

The militant nodded and stood, motioning for several of the men to follow.

"If we can take the east walk and the armoury, we have the superior position and can turn their weapons against them," said Jabir.

"The armoury is too heavily defended. Come up with another suggestion or fall back and fight another day," said Shepard.

Jabir held his left arm low against his side and Shepard noticed blood trickling down the man's wrist.

"Are you hit?"

"It is nothing."

"Bullshit. Let me see?"

Jabir moved his arm. Blood soaked from the armpit all the way to the waistband of his pants. As he moved, Shepard saw him wince and knew that he'd taken a clean shot. He was a tough son of a bitch to still be on his feet and contemplating a push on the armoury.

"Where are your friends?"

Shepard shook his head. He had managed to get a weak signal to TAC and offer a brief update to Canning and Porter that both he and the asset were safe but about to engage in an assault with rebel forces against a Russian/militia stronghold.

Canning's words had been choice and Porter had offered a stark assessment on getting any form of help. They had agreed on a drone which would likely be unarmed to provide live, from the air, tactical updates. All in all, about as much use as an ashtray in an Apache gunship.

"Nothing. We don't have the authority to engage a pro-government base." He shrugged.

Jabir spat blood on the dirt.

"You fight well, Captain. It is a shame they tie your hands. Perhaps another time we could have seen off the oppressors before it ever got to this." Jabir reached out and slapped Shepard's shoulder.

"Bashir? Tariq?" He called two of his men closer.

"Captain, I am going to Allah and I am taking as many of these godless bastards as possible with me. You will lead the rest of these men to take the armoury and snatch us victory from the jaws of defeat."

"Jabir…" Shepard started, unsure how to persuade the man on a different course.

"Has your father not lost enough today?" said Feriha. "Have you not lost enough?" She gestured towards the killing ground beyond their cover. Above, Qusay and his men traded shots with the closing Russians and militia infantry.

Jabir smiled. There was blood on his teeth.

"Child, there is no life for any of us as long as our land is not free. I know this in my heart, my father taught it and he would give his life likewise. I am sorry…"

"Don't be sorry. Fall back. Regroup…"

"I am sorry I did not listen to you. Perhaps, if you had been allowed to get your evidence out, the Americans could have helped us. Now we will never know," said Jabir.

They flinched at the zip of incoming rounds. Shepard, arms wide, shooed both of them into deeper cover. Backing them up against the stony mesh block then sweeping his carbine up and sighting the shooter, he fired off two quick shots. Both missed as the man ducked behind a shattered concrete traffic block.

Anticipating the coming movement, Shepard dropped the red dot aim-point onto the edge of the block, wavering left to right. As the head rose to fire Shepard's single shot struck him in the face. The body crumpled out of sight.

"They are closing," Qusay shouted from his vantage point, kneeling below the exposed lip to reload. Jabir gave a wave of acknowledgement.

"You must make ready."

"Jabir…"

"He's right," said Shepard.

"No…"

"Even if we could make the tunnels and they don't collapse them on top of us, they'll launch an offensive into the city and bomb us to bits. The only way out is to keep fighting."

Feriha made to speak but Shepard stalled her.

"The plan is the same. Just stick with me. I'll take the armoury, Jabir." He faced the Syrian commander and nodded at the group of men behind. "I have an idea for a counter-attack, have the rest of your men fall in and be ready to storm the building. We'll secure a firebase and push out from there."

"What about the technicals and armour? We'll never get past them," said Feriha. Jabir's and Shepard's reckless optimism that the plan had a chance of succeeding eluded her.

Jabir smiled and then was wracked by a hacking cough. When he composed himself, he was paler, but his expression peaceful.

"Leave that to me."

Chapter 25

Khalid Al-Salam sprinted forward and unloaded the remaining rounds of his Soviet RPK at the militants on the ridge of protective blocks. To his left and right, his men swarmed forward, weaving through the cover afforded by the heavy machine-gun fire that zipped and cracked overhead from the technicals and Yegorov's BTR.

The Russian troops were similarly bounding forward on the right flank and within the next minutes, they would have the militants' position fixed between their lines of fire.

He twisted the weapon and let off a long burst as three of the terrorists sprinted from cover to take up a new firing position. Dropping to his knee, he tracked a fourth as he ran, leading the man until the last second. The flare of muzzle flash robbed him of his vision, but enough remained to see the man fall. He reloaded, snapping a fresh magazine home.

Rising to his feet and firing into the air, Khalid screamed for his men to advance.

❖

Yegorov bounced in the hatch of the BTR as it circled back around to take another run along the offensive line the attackers had stubbornly refused to relinquish.

Tactically, it was a poor choice of position. Narrow and

with the only exits covered by the heavy-bore weapons of the BTR and the technicals, it would soon become a kill zone as his own troops and those of Al-Waleed closed enough to begin lobbing grenades and launching an assault down the single channel that ran along its length.

He depressed the triggers of the .50-cal. The rounds ripped into the Hesco barrier that offered shelter, doing no damage to those sheltered behind but sending chunks of rock and debris scattering to the sky and keeping heads pinned down as tracer ricocheted into the sky.

As he traversed the weapon back across he caught sight of Khalid Al-Salam as he cut down a runner and then stood, firing into the air and urging his men on

❖

Shepard gave Feriha a confident nod and beckoned her closer.

Above, on the parapet, chunks of debris blasted loose. Qusay and his men hunkered down as a new onslaught from the heavy machine guns battered their precarious position.

"Be ready." He gave her arm a quick squeeze and then slung his carbine behind him and clambered up onto the barricade and scooted across to Qusay. He leaned in and shouted in the man's ear.

The noise of the incoming rounds was deafening.

"You ready?"

"I am ready, Northern Ireland."

Shepard nodded and put two fingers in the air to call time. Qusay smiled, barked orders, and his men backed up to the wall, ready to crest.

A small Syrian with rotten front teeth grinned as he squeezed in beside Shepard. He tugged open the collar of his jacket to reveal a red jersey underneath.

"Man United. George Best. Number one!"

Shepard laughed in spite of the situation.

"Let them have the craic!" The Syrian slapped him on the leg and then picked up a weapon.

From his position, Shepard had a view along the protective path to where Jabir and his two men prepared to exit into the maelstrom. Risking a quick peep above he saw the fan of enemy troops break and begin their run across the open ground between the tarmac and the gravel perimeter track. Ducking back down, he grabbed the offered weapon from Qusay's man on his left and jumped up.

"NOW!"

❖

Khalid Al-Salam was running full tilt when the heads appeared over the protective wall. Firing from the hip as he sprinted across the open ground, his rounds were largely ineffectual as the men clambered higher above their defensive position.

His RPK stammered to click empty and as he reached for a new magazine, the first whooshing trails of the RPGs arced down to meet his troop's line of advance.

❖

Yegorov's head snapped round ninety degrees as the first impact rumbled across the compound. The BTR lumbered through a turn before lining up to race back across the wall. As he shifted to bring the .50-cal to bear, the whooshing trails of ten rocket-propelled grenades streaked down to detonate in the ranks of the advancing infantry.

The booming explosions continued as each rocket struck home, swirling smoke and divots of debris clearing to reveal writhing bodies.

He couldn't see any sign of Khalid. The area where he had led his charge was now levelled by the barrage of high explosive grenades.

Focused fire began to rain in from the left and right edges of the defensive wall. Rounds zinged off the APC's reinforced bodywork.

Yegorov thumbed his mic.

"Give them no room to regroup. All units. Open fire."

Chapter 26

Shepard dropped the firing tube and twisted to receive a fresh RPG from Feriha.

She ducked low and away from the exhaust as he settled the launcher on his shoulder and dropped the iron sights on a technical racing parallel to the wall towards where Jabir and his two men had spread out and were sprinting towards the gathering pocket of vehicles racing away from the surprise RPG attack. Distracted by the contrails and explosions, they hadn't noticed the approaching militants.

As one technical bounced down onto the tarmac of the plateau its gunner spotted the men and he tracked his machine gun to open up on the trio. As the rounds chewed up the ground between them, Shepard loosed the rocket.

The ignition booster hissed to life as he squeezed the trigger and, with a familiar whoosh, the grenade left the launch tube, stabiliser fins popping into place. After a dozen metres a tiny piezoelectric fuse popped the squib of nitro and the rocket caught a second wind, racing forward to its maximum velocity of three hundred feet per second.

The rocket's tail of bluish-white smoke spiralled as it streaked down towards the vehicle. The gunner caught sight and yelled a warning but the driver was too slow to react. The two-kilo warhead struck the jeep behind the cab and exploded.

The gunner pinwheeled through the air, his clothes and hair on fire. Ablaze and out of control, the jeep swerved and struck another head on as it weaved around a set of concrete blocking pillars to escape the second volley. The gunner of the second vehicle was thrown free, his leg snapping violently as he hit the ground.

Shepard dropped the second launcher and snatched up his carbine, preparing to move.

In the distance, he could see the injured man, howls of pain dying on his lips as Jabir's assault rifle picked him out, rattling a dozen rounds into the writhing body.

Bashir and Tariq vaulted the metal traffic barrier separating the gravel track and the road and ran towards the headlights of the approaching vehicles. The ground around and under them was pricked by exploding shells, but miraculously both men zigzagged through the storm.

The lead vehicle swerved to take them head on, a second jerking out of line behind to form a speeding barrier of steel. Both men sprayed their Kalashnikovs on full auto at the oncoming jeeps. Windshields popped with impacts and sparks bounced off door pillars and wheel arches as the vehicles sped forward to bury the militants under their wheels.

Both men were fully illuminated in the headlights; they were ten yards away. Too close to avoid. Shepard winced at the flash which came a split second before the tremulous boom which rumbled across the compound.

Bashir triggered his vest a heartbeat before Tariq and thirty pounds of high explosive and wads of shrapnel-packed material expanded from where they had stood, shredding the first vehicles. White-hot shrapnel tore through fuel lines and gas tanks, the two vehicles flipping on their axles as they exploded, adding to the thunder that rippled across the plateau.

Jabir's rapid advance was slowing. His right arm pressed tight on his stomach and his left leg was dragging.

He flopped across the metal barrier and walked into the roadway, sensing the impending danger, head jerking around as lights washed over him.

Shepard could only watch as the BTR screeched around the corner and buried the Syrian under its wide wheelbase.

The initial impact knocked Jabir six yards ahead of the APC, throwing him from his feet, tearing his weapon free, and cartwheeling him in an awkward tumble. The roar of the BTR's four hundred horsepower grunted as it rolled over the top of the militant commander.

Shepard could see the glee on the top gunner's face and then the shock as Jabir's explosive vest detonated below the soft underbelly of the big beast.

❖

Shepard jumped from the height of the Hesco barricade to the ground and swept his Colt carbine from the sling and up into firing position.

There was only one way to go now. It was uncomplicated and as straightforward a military manoeuvre as had ever been sketched in the book; a full on, full frontal blitz.

Feriha joined him, followed by half a dozen of Qusay's fighters. The Syrian commander and the rest of his men continued to pour fire down on the disorientated and scrambling defenders as they tried to regroup and assist casualties from the devastation of the three suicide bombs.

Shepard took off at a run, the group running in a phalanx behind. The assault would need to be swift, and it would need to be brutal to take full advantage of the chaos.

The Russian troops who had been establishing positions to storm the trench line were in disarray. A burning jeep was buried under the tarps of the mess tent and the entire structure was on fire.

Beyond that the BTR was intact, but its bodywork buckled, the front wheels splayed out at right angles. Smoke poured from the top hatch.

As he sprinted from cover, Shepard raised the Colt carbine and picked out his first target. The man's mouth formed an O of surprise just as the first .223 round hit him in the throat.

The man beside him fell next, a thumbprint sized impact to his forehead, and a red cloud from the exit wound burst from the back of his skull.

The rest of the raid line opened fire. It was far from textbook, but it was working. Shepard picked targets to his front, snapping off rounds and counting them down as they hit home. Feriha took the arc to his left, the man beside her, the arc to his right. Each slice of the pie covered. Alternating with each man in the line. The last man responsible for covering them all.

Shepard had drilled the men assigned to him before the rocket attack on what he expected. Single rounds or focused bursts. They had neither the manpower nor the ammunition to spray and pray. To a man, they were following through.

Ahead, the Russian troops collected themselves but their undisciplined panicked fire went wildly overhead or stitched in the dirt around the assault teams' feet.

Shepard dropped his aim-point on another militiaman and sent him spinning to the ground with two to the chest. As he swept left, he noticed one of the Russian non-coms taking charge. He was bellowing orders. Organising a skirmish line. Physically pulling men from cover to fight back.

Shepard sighted down-range on the run, the man's mouth moving in the frame of the ACOG scope, the face twisted in fury as his men crumbled under pressure. Shepard's first round struck him on the helmet, the bullet zinging off with a spark and the target twisted away. His next four rounds zipped along the seam of the sergeant's body armour, by the time the fifth struck he had crumpled to the floor and the men were in full rout.

Ahead, the armoury loomed. They were closing fast on the hangar-style building. Qusay's men still poured out automatic fire and an occasional whoosh and crump of RPG thumped into the militia holding the comms centre.

Shepard led his team around a cinderblock building, sweeping ninety degrees left at full pace and straight into the axis of a squad of militia. Concentrated on the chaos of the plateau, the first man didn't notice. Shepard was twenty feet away when he squeezed off a round to hit the man flush in the side of the head, his body dropping like a stone. The movement caused the second man in line to turn, catching Shepard's next round between the eyes.

The third militiaman had eyes wide on the approach of the raiders but was having a harder time bringing his weapon to bear.

Having counted out the last round, Shephard dropped the Colt to its three-point sling and pulled the pistol from his chest holster, extending his arm and shooting the man through the bridge of the nose. As he hurdled the falling body, he shot the next guard in the face and then, stepping high over the corpse, he reached out, grabbing the last man by the collar and twisting him against the wall of the armoury building. Shoving the muzzle of the 9mm USP into the struggling man's back, he sent two shots through his spine and into his heart.

❖

Dimitri Yegorov booted open the rear doors of the APC and spilled out into a heap. His first breath caught as he exhaled the toxic smoke that had filled the cabin, his lung lining seared from the heat of the blast that had lifted the big carrier off its wheelbase and slammed it down like a child's toy.

Gritting his teeth, Yegorov tried to stand, but the pain made him gasp and triggered a bout of fitful half coughs. Eventually, he sucked in a clean breath and grabbed the rear step of the carrier to pull himself up. A dead soldier was half hanging out of the troop compartment, the driver was slumped over the steering wheel.

Yegorov's legs were numb, and he shook his head to dissipate the ringing in his ears, the movement sending him to his knees, his L1 to L5 lumbar burning. The impact of the blast had driven the seat of the .50-cal turret upwards, slamming his sacrum into the upper vertebrae. He'd suffered back pain before following training and parachute accidents, but nothing like this.

All around was chaos as his own, and the remnants of the Al-Waleed forces scrambled to put up a defence. It shouldn't have come to this. He shouldn't have let it come to this. The hammer of the Soviet military should have slammed down on the insurgents. Shock and awe should have killed the militants' appetite to fight, but his arrogance had got the better of him. He'd wanted to see their shock, the surprise as he opened the jaws of the trap and slammed it closed behind them.

He wrested an AK-74 from the grip of a dead soldier and stumbled around the carcass of the APC. Ahead, the tangled mess of two technicals burned. The mantis-like corpse of the driver blackened in the cab. The crack-crack-crack of rounds cooking off in the fires split the air and added to bursts of gunfire that rippled across the compound.

To his right, a small unit of men was in cover, trading sporadic bursts with a knot of Khalid Al-Salam's militia.

To his left, a line of the terrorists charged from swirling smoke towards the armoury, the man leading them scything through a line of defenders as though they weren't there and to his left, a woman. Yegorov grunted and felt anger and adrenaline flood in to dull the pain. The soldier who had fled like a rat into the ruins with the spy. He took a few wobbling steps towards a line of his men hunkered in the cover of the cinder block ablutions.

He wasn't about to suffer defeat from a ragtag rabble of so-called freedom fighters with home-made explosives. Nor was he about to let the spy and her western rescuer escape unhindered.

Not when he had one last ace up his sleeve.

Chapter 27

"…three!"

Feriha, finger on the trigger guard of her AKM, barrel pointed at the deck, reached across with her free hand and jerked the door open.

Shepard went first, flipping the lever of the fragmentation grenade and tumbling the explosive through the open portal. Two more of the raid line mirrored his action right after, each man twisting away to take shelter against the blockwork wall of the armoury building.

The three dull crumps echoed in quick succession. Debris and smoke billowed out of the open door.

"Go. Go. Go!"

Shepard took point through the door, sighting a wounded fighter bringing his weapon to bear, and squeezing off two shots which stuck home and propelled the man backwards over crates of armaments. He popped the sights of his weapon back up, searching for targets, and they raced to clear the building.

The line broke into three sections as they charged inside. Shepard's orders had been firm, storm the space from front to back, aggression over accuracy, eliminate the defenders, secure the cache.

Shepard charged ahead with Feriha at his shoulder. He had

prepared for a space of tall racks and narrow channels of stacked equipment that would be a nightmare to scrap through, but the area was far more open than he had expected though no less lightly defended.

A grenade boomed as the militants stormed down the right-hand flank. Gunfire blazed in return and he caught sight of one of his allies spin away, wounded. A series of low crates dominated the floor space while along the edges and stacked higher were tall wooden crates, Arabic writing on one edge, Chinese on the other. Beyond that, on each side, a metal staircase rose to a gantry and mezzanine floor. Along the chain-link safety rail and protected by low metal containers and jute sacks, heads jerked out of cover followed by the telltale flash of incoming. A waspish buzz sped past his ear, thwacking into a stack of the crates and darting his cheek with splinters. Setting his sights on the higher ground, he fired off a sustained burst, sending the heads ducking back to cover.

Shepard raced across the floor space to the foot of the stairs and bounded the steps three at a time, the stairway quivering under the impact of his footfalls and the echo of Feriha's sprint evident by the vibrations from behind. Cresting, he swept right to be blinded by muzzle flare and the heat of 7.62mm rounds as they flashed by his face. The Russian rose higher for a second attempt. Rounds drilled into the soldier's sternum as Feriha unloaded, blasting him into his comrade whose aim had been tracking Shepard.

Shepard fired a single round, the headshot tumbling the soldier over the rail to the floor below.

"Left!" Shepard chopped a hand and Feriha followed his order. Shepard took the right channel.

The upper section of the armoury was divided into two corridors of packed racking. Same crates. Same writing. At five-metre intervals, cross paths split the channel. From ahead, the second intersection along, a flash of uniform, then the distinct clink, clank, clank of metal on metal.

He spotted the grenade as it tumbled forward in a jerky, bouncing roll. The channel offered no protection.

Shepard ticked off the milliseconds as he closed in, sweeping a boot at the explosive to tumble it left under the racking and using his momentum to launch himself right. He slammed into the face of the intersection and scrambled for cover as the grenade exploded. The explosion and zipping bite of shrapnel were suppressed by the storage crates and shelving.

Not waiting for a repeat, he was up and moving. Spotted the arm ahead draw back. Gritting his teeth and driving forward, he raised the carbine, seeking the target as he ran, rewarded as a sliver of body eased into view. Depressing the trigger, Shepard emptied the rest of the magazine, catching sight of the first three impacts. Thigh. Groin. Stomach. He sprinted on as he watched the figure fall, hands snatching for purchase but a grenade tumbling into their lap. The detonation blew chunks of flesh, wooden packaging, and shards of racks in a plume of smoke and burning metal across the intersection.

Gunfire raged to his left and then went quiet.

Ahead, the mezzanine opened out and the rear stairs descended to the main floor.

Feriha eased around the corner, alert and unscathed.

"Clear?" said Shepard.

"Clear."

❖

"Captain?"

Shepard descended the stairs to find Jabir's militants gathered in a loose defensive formation.

"Ahmed." Shepard nodded a sombre greeting. "Upstairs is

clear. Are we secure down here?"

"Yes, sir." The militant was the small Manchester United supporter with the rotten teeth. His face was set in a concerned frown.

"Casualties?"

"We have men wounded, but there is a bigger problem."

Shepard dropped his carbine to its sling and glanced around the group. The men who were functioning seemed alert and vigilant. One of the number was assessing a group of four wounded, and Feriha slung her weapon and moved to assist. Of the four, his keen eyes told him two would live, one would likely lose his leg, and the other would be dead in the next fifteen minutes.

"Get the men ready to repel a counter-attack and have some of these crates broken open to see what we can use. Look for RPGs or anti-vehicle weapons. They still have technicals and God knows what other armour."

Ahmed barked the order in his native tongue and the men ordered themselves into groups, one to scavenge for munitions and another setting up to repel the almost assured counter-attack.

"What is it?"

Ahmed cocked his index finger and bade Shepard to follow.

As soon as he graced the leading edge of the racking which had blocked his view of the armoury loading bay, he saw the problem.

To the right, an area had been sealed off with rudimentary screens and plastic sheeting, through which Shepard could see racks of 155mm ordnance. Outside this, there were barrels stacked five by five and five again high and there had to be at least ten of the pallets. The sight was reminiscent of a well-stocked beer store with one horrific exception.

Each of the sealed barrels carried a skull and crossbones

and perhaps even more chilling, a triangle of interlocking dots that designated the cargo as contravening the April '97 United Nations Chemical Weapons Convention.

As he was wrapping his mind around the connotations of the discovery, Shepard felt his blood run cold.

Six feet away, beside a four-by-four-metre section of desks and filing cabinets, a corkboard was pinned with sections of map.

Each map had an acetate overlay of concentric circles shaded lighter the further away from the bullseye they fell. Scrawled in the margins were figures and notations for windage and dispersal rate and along the bottom margin estimated casualty rates.

Chapter 28

Dimitri Yegorov half walked and half stumbled with his small group of men from the ablutions to a covered vehicle bay. Blood dripped from his left ear and his teeth were on edge as he bit down to suppress the grind of vertebrae with each step.

The vehicle bay was a general-purpose maintenance area where the assigned crews could strip the vehicles for minor repair, jury-rig faults, and clean the sand and dust that clogged the air filters and carburettors and eroded the moving parts of the engines.

"That one and that one." Yegorov assigned his men to drop two of the Tigr armoured jeeps from their ramps and make them ready for use. Each of the five-ton jeeps were in stages of repair; both hoods up, one had a wheel missing, the other a complete wing and front grille. Importantly though, the 30mm cannon atop the first and the 40mm grenade launcher on the second were fully functional.

"Get the munitions out and set up a base plate there." Yegorov rested against a bench of scattered parts and tools. He looked across the compound at the steady progress of the terrorists pushing Al-Salam's men back to the command post. On the other side, the sounds of explosions and gunfire were muffled within the armoury building. He would not sacrifice the compound to the enemy, and neither would he allow the armoury's contents to become a bargaining chip to force a tactical withdrawal of his forces.

If he couldn't hold the ground no one would.

"Zero on the armoury. HE rounds."

"Colonel?" The trooper looked up quizzically as he thumbed the wing nuts of the mortar tube to the baseplate stand.

"You heard me. Volley fire of three rounds, walking front to back. Standby for my command."

"But, sir? The shells? The barrel bombs? We'll be killed too."

Yegorov awkwardly pulled his Makarov and aimed it at the trooper, his eyes wild in fury and pain.

"I'll kill you now myself if you don't do as I say, trooper!" Spittle flecked from the Russian's lips.

The trooper ducked his head and continued to make the mortar ready. One of the Tigr's bounced on its axles as it slammed off the ramp. In the hatch, another soldier primed the grenade launcher.

Yegorov wiped his mouth, his teeth bloody as he grinned at the hell he was about to rain down on his enemy.

❖

"Did Jabir know about this?"

"I... I don't know," said Ahmed.

"You don't know or you don't want to tell me?"

Shepard stood up from a crouch and looked around. Ahmed's men had found a box of Chinese Type 69 85mm rocket-propelled grenades and were handballing them to the front shutter of the armoury, where it was likely the militia/Russian troops would scale an assault. Not that any defence was going to be up to much if a stray round caught the cache of chemical weapons.

Like all British forces engaged in the years of fighting

across the Middle East and beyond, he had received the CBRN drills. The teams had fought and practised extensively in the heavy, uncomfortable containment suits as the threat of chemical and biological warfare edged more towards reality than nightmare and he'd only slightly trusted the kit would protect him from a horrific and painful certain death.

Standing this close to enough of the stuff to strip twenty square miles of biological life was making his skin crawl. He loosed his ballistic helmet, taking it off and running a hand through sweat-soaked hair.

"What is this?"

Feriha strode across the floor, eased aside a section of the sheeting, and then her gaze fell on the barrel bombs.

"It's not good," said Shepard. "I'd say we've just found the payload that gassed the village and by the look of it they hadn't planned to stop there."

He indicated the corkboard.

The first map showed the rebel-held areas of Maghrabad under the chilling acetate of the chemical weapon fallout estimate. The second map showed Al-Tanf airbase.

"Are you able to take a guess at what we are looking at?"

Feriha cast widening eyes across the stockpile.

"The footage from Misraa showed the victims suffering vomiting and asphyxiation. I don't know exactly, perhaps some complex compound of diphosgene and a chlorine derivative?"

"If I rig charges to blow it, will we make matters worse?"

"I'm not an expert, but I would think that if the initial blast wasn't big enough, it could disperse whatever wasn't destroyed. I don't think it's a risk we want to take."

"That's what I thought. Right, Ahmed. Tell your men we need to break out of this box, it's not a position we want to be caught trying to defend."

Shepard took a step away and emptied a jute sack of

7.62mm rounds onto the floor, then passed it across to Feriha.

"Grab all you can from the corkboard and off those tables. This is a stockpile, not a manufacturing centre. If we're lucky, once the spooks start to trawl through, it'll lead somewhere."

He put his ballistic helmet back on and checked his weapons. They were in for another fight breaking out of the armoury and he wasn't sure if this time it was one they would win.

Ahmed and his men were loading up the RPG warheads and dragging boxes of grenades to divide between them when Shepard heard the dull crump.

"Incoming!"

The mortar round exploded thirty feet short of the front entrance, obliterating a parked-up forklift and small Portakabin, the blast close enough to shower the militants with the debris.

"Whatever you can fit in the sack. Leave the rest," he said.

Feriha nodded, sweeping sheaves of paper and notes from the tabletops.

Shepard ran to Ahmed.

Two more crumps of mortar in quick succession. They both landed further to the east of the building than the first.

The Syrian was peering through the smoke of the first explosion.

"He is shit shot."

Shepard followed the militant's gaze. Something bright wavered in the gloom beyond the cloud of soot and smoke from the destroyed temporary cabin and loader.

"Maybe he knows what will happen if he lands one on top of us."

A draught of warm air crossing the city from the plains coiled the black smoke into a rising column and Shepard caught sight of the Tigr jeeps roaring towards them an instant before the top-mounted grenade launcher opened up with a throaty pap-pap-pap-pap.

Chapter 29

Shepard felt a hand on the strap of his webbing and the friction of his backside dragging across the floor. His hearing had gone and then slowly noises began to register on the low scale first. Dull persistent vibrations then the accelerating rush of treble and finally the thump of deep bass as explosions and gunfire zipped around him.

"Are you okay?" Feriha leaned over him. He could read her lips, but the words were jumbled.

Above her, Ahmed emptied the magazine of his AK-74 and then bent to pick up a Type 69 rocket launcher.

"I'm fine. I'm okay."

Shepard pulled himself to a knee as another barrage of grenades hit the side of the armoury building, bringing a broad sheet of corrugated metal and blockwork tumbling down in a cloud of dust and flame.

Ahmed settled into his stance and loosed the RPG out through the enormous gap torn in the front of the building by the initial grenade salvo.

Shepard shook off the cobwebs of concussion and moved forward, feeling a weakness in his right leg. There was no blood, and it didn't feel broken, so perhaps just an awkward landing as the shockwave of the blast had pitched him backwards.

Another RPG streaked out and hit one of the jeeps, the rocket detonating but the vehicle's armour holding. They had set themselves up on each side of the entrance, each covering the arc of the other.

Shepard raised his carbine and set the aim-point. The barrel lifted with the three-round burst and as the sight fell back he was rewarded with the view of the gunner slumped over the lip of the top hatch.

The ground around his feet shattered and sparked as the 30mm cannon of the second Tigr poured gunfire into the building. As Shepard scrambled right, he watched as the dead gunner was hauled into the cabin and a second man racked the launcher.

"Neptune. Neptune. This is Coyote Six. Copy?"

Under the heavy suppression provided by the two vehicles, the swarming movement of infantry flitted through the smoky haze. Shepard tracked the lead soldier, let him close, and then let him have an aimed burst to the chest. The second man he caught too high to be fatal, but the force dropped him behind the rubble of the shattered entrance.

"Coyote. Solid copy. Good to hear a friendly voice," said Shepard, a shiver of exhilaration running through him at the prospect that Canning or Porter had succeeded in bending the rules of engagement.

"Roger, Neptune, standby."

Shepard slid another RPG across to Ahmed, who was buried under a sustained burst of heavy-bore cannon. Moving to a crouch and then running to a sprint, Shepard raced across the floor, snapping off shots at the advancing infantry until the heavy cannon tracked towards him.

Rounds shattered the racks and equipment boxes as he slid behind the cover of a concrete-encased support beam. The whoosh of Ahmed's RPG drowned out the sound of the cannon. A detonation, but no cessation to the incoming rounds.

"Neptune, Coyote on final approach and ready for tasking."

"Coyote. Troops in contact. Blue in the superstructure south-east side of the compound. Multiple enemy vehicles and infantry outside."

"Neptune. Copy. Confirm visual. Standby for fire."

Shepard slid around his cover and aimed at a duo of infantry who had penetrated the hangar and were in a flanking position to Ahmed's men. His first shot was true, and the soldier fell. The second was nowhere near.

Outside, the ground lit up with incoming fire as the AH-64 Apache gunship swooped low over the plateau and unleashed its nose-mounted M23 chain gun. The 30mm rounds chewed up the tarmac between the two Tigrs, studding the rightmost jeep along the side panel. As smoke and sparks poured from the hatch, the rushing whoosh of incoming rockets roared in.

The heat of the impacting Hydra 70mm unguided rockets blasted into the armoury, the vehicle and the mouth of the building enveloped in flame and scattering debris.

"Good hit, Coyote."

"Roger. Neptune, be advised, infantry massing on your six."

As the surviving Tigr roared to life, Shepard made his way back across the floor to Feriha, Ahmed and the remaining fighters, spotting the jeep disgorge a cargo of soldiers then move from the wreckage of its partner to find cover from the air support.

"Troops coming in from the rear," said Shepard, taking a knee and beckoning them close.

"We exit out the front. We have support in the air for the minute."

"Neptune. Neptune, this is Rickshaw One-Four. We are on

approach to open ground two hundred metres west of your position. Copy?" Haley Adam's voice was as cool as ever.

"Appreciate the lift, Haley. Copy that. I have seven passengers."

Ahmed gripped him on the arm and shook his head, holding up two fingers.

"My place is here, Northern Ireland. We will cover you."

Shepard nodded. From the other side of the compound came a rumble of thunder and then the roiling cloud of flame and smoke as the command centre exploded.

"Qusay," said Ahmed, stumps of teeth on display as he grinned.

"Haley, scratch last. Two passengers, standby."

"Roger, Neptune. One minute out."

Coyote made another pass above the front of the armoury, chain gun stitching across the cowering remainder of Russian and militia troops.

"You ready?"

Feriha nodded.

Shepard slapped Ahmed's arm and turned to lead the way out.

Chapter 30

As the Merlin banked over the rooftops of the shattered city, Haley Adams dialled back the speed to just over a hundred miles per hour, the chaos of battle raging directly ahead bathed in green tinge and white flare as she surveyed her route to the LZ through her popped down NVGs.

The helicopter dipped and bucked as it swept across the outlying parkland.

"Neptune. Thirty seconds," said Adams. "Trident, prepare to land. We have two passengers."

Mark Mills, Token, and Gash carried an arsenal of weapons between them. Mills on the left an FN Minimi 5.62mm SAW light machine gun, Token the standard C8 carbine, and Gash had a larger M60 GPMG lashed on a strap in the open door and aimed down at the ground rushing below.

All three troopers and the Merlin crew had their NVGs popped down and were ready for a noisy welcome on the ground.

"One-Four. Troops in the open. Left, left, left," said Mills.

Below, a group of twenty soldiers were moving from the burning wreckage of a block and wood building to the treeline.

"Copy, Trident. Do you have eyes on Neptune?"

Haley Adams took her final turn, a sweeping left-hand

bank that dropped the Merlin to a hundred feet.

Flame and smoke rushed up and over the windshield, the rotors coiling it away in violent black contrails.

"Eyes on. Right," said Gash.

Adams risked a glance out the side window. She spotted the two runners moving from the wreck of a large structure and tracking to intercept her at the LZ.

Gash swung the M60 to track motion. Racked the big machine gun and thumbed his comms.

"Neptune. Trident. One-Four. Enemy closing right, right, right! No shot. No shot."

❖

Shepard was flagging, and Feriha was struggling behind. He could hear the thunderous roar of the Merlin as it dropped in towards the clearing.

The zip of incoming and the ricochet of rounds thunking wood and scattering leaves preceded Gash's warning shout across the net.

Swinging his weapon to bear, Shepard dropped the red dot aim-point on the first trooper who came rushing from the trees, the burst catching the man in a tight group around the heart.

Switching left, he sent another two rounds into the face of the next soldier. As he swapped back right, Feriha tripped, sprawling headlong in the dirt.

Shepard stopped and fired a blind burst towards the nearest muzzle flash, feeling a round as it tugged the shoulder of his BDUs and another zip past his ear. Then he was on his backside as a ricochet clipped his helmet.

Feriha was back on her feet and lugging the laptop bag and jute sack of intel as he rose to a knee, shaking the ringing from his ears.

A soldier closed in, taking aim. Shepard fired a three-round burst. Target down. Switch to the next. Double tap. Target down.

Feriha caught back up to him as the downwash of the Merlin passed directly overhead.

Gunfire from behind pushed the attackers to hit the ground or scramble behind trees as Ahmed's men offered additional support.

The blinking lights of Haley Adam's bird strobed through the trees, grass and branches caught in the hurricane of the spinning rotor wash.

They were fifty metres away. He could see Gash in the door and Mark Mills and Token leap out onto the grass.

Shepard reached out to drag Feriha on when a shadow swept in from his right and sent him sprawling to the ground.

As he felt the body land heavily on top of him, a second pair of arms wrapped themselves around Feriha.

He saw her throw her head back, smashing into the man's face as a Makarov barrel pressed down on the bridge of his own nose.

❖

Shepard's right hand palmed the forearm aiming the pistol away as Dimitri Yegorov squeezed the trigger.

The shot went off like a firecracker, its report agonisingly loud in his ear and the muzzle flash blinding.

Snarling, the Russian fought against the firm grip on his wrist and squeezed off a second round which thudded into the earth a foot from Shepard's head.

His left arm was pinned by the Russian's right and he flailed his feet to find purchase and buck the man loose, managing to prise one heel into the ground and force his hips up.

The movement drove the man on top off his chest only for him to come crashing back down with a wheezing gasp of pain, knocking the breath from Shepard as he landed.

The grip on Shepard's arm loosened, and he swung a blind haymaker that connected with the Russian's ear. Yegorov's head rocked, but the imbalance had gained him control of Shepard's right hand.

He swept the Makarov forward, squeezing off a third shot.

Shepard jerked his head left. Then right, as a fourth round buried into the ground inches from his head. Bucking his hips again, he flipped the Russian and momentum carried them both over.

Yegorov roared in agony and anger, as his legs propelled both feet into Shepard's chest. As he raised the gun, Shepard kicked out, his heavy boot striking the Russian on the scaphoid and knocking the pistol from his grip.

Shepard pulled his USP from the chest holster.

Feriha screamed.

Her attacker had lifted her into the air, her feet freewheeling in front of her as the soldier grappled to contain her with one hand and draw his weapon with the other.

Shepard snapped the pistol out and fired off a single shot.

Blood bloomed from the soldier's cheek, and both he and Feriha collapsed to the dirt.

Gunfire zipped in from the direction of the Merlin.

Gash and Mills were on the move.

Shepard swept the USP back towards the Russian, his aim thrown as pain exploded across his knee cap, the joint collapsing under a savage strike. A second bright flash of pain as another kick scraped down his shin.

The Russian scrambled for his own weapon.

Shepard allowed his bodyweight to take him to the ground, a stab of pain blooming as he rolled onto his left shoulder. The Russian swept up his gun and took aim.

Shepard fired first, the 9mm round catching the man in the thigh. The Makarov barked, but the aim was wide.

Shepard fired again.

The Russian stumbled as the bullet buried in his gut. His weapon hand wavered as he sighted on Shepard.

Shepard's next shot took him in the teeth and exited in a gory grey-red haze out the back of his skull.

As he tumbled backwards, Shepard felt hands grabbing him and snapped out a hand to break the grip.

"It's Gash, boss. Up. Up. Up."

Shepard allowed the SBS trooper to help him stand. He stopped to grab the jute sack from the armoury and almost fell as a lightning rod of pain flooded down his left arm and from his knee through his fibula.

Gash took the sack and his weight and, as they turned, he watched Mark Mills hoist Feriha off the ground.

Token took a knee and smashed a fusillade of rounds through the trees at the remaining Russians.

Shepard limped heavily forward, eyes on Mills' back. The trooper's weapon was slung, the rucksack in one hand, the woman flopping limply across his shoulders. Feriha's eyes were closed and blood dripped from her chin down Mills' BDUs.

As the crew chief dragged him aboard the Merlin, Haley Adam's keyed her mic and fed power to the Rolls Royce turboshaft engines, the Merlin lurching skywards.

"One-Four. All call signs. Neptune is feet dry. Package secure."

Shepard felt his stomach lurch at the sudden elevation and heard the pop-pop-pop of chaff as Adams fired off the defence measures and put the bird into a hard banking turn, the motion throwing Shepard against the bulkhead next to Feriha. Kestrel's face was pale. Mills was beside her, ripping open her shirt.

Yegorov's last stray round had missed Shepard by a mile, but it had found a target.

Epilogue

"Is she going to be alright?"

"No thanks to you."

Shepard popped his sunglasses up onto the top of his head and winced as he tried to sit up on the lounger.

"You're welcome," he said, raising a hand to shade his eyes.

Christmas Porter stepped into the glare of the sun and offered over a bottle of Coors Light beer.

"Am I supposed to be drinking while I'm on the meds?"

Porter laughed as she slumped into the lawn chair next to him and clinked the neck of her bottle against his.

"I always said you lot should stick to the water. You're too slow on land."

Shepard grunted and took a long draught of the beer. He looked up, surprised.

"Corky had a pallet shipped out. He has a stash in the hangar for emergencies." Porter took a sip of her drink and raised her face to the late afternoon sun.

"You sure you're okay?" she said.

"I'm fine, Porter. It's a scratch."

"The doc said otherwise." Porter poked a finger into the wadding of bandage that wrapped Shepard's shoulder, his left arm immobilised by a sling. He jerked back from the jab.

"I didn't even feel it until I got into the chopper," he said.

He figured he'd been hit when Feriha had fallen. He remembered clearly the tug at his shoulder and the clip on the helmet, but after that, the sudden adrenaline rush of his fight with the Russian must have numbed the shock of being shot.

"She's definitely okay?"

"You sweet on her, Shepard?" Christmas Porter narrowed her eyes.

"You jealous?"

"She'll be fine. Round went straight through and apart from the break, missed anything vital. It was a lucky shot."

Shepard thought back to how different it could have been. As Adams took the bird skywards, Mills and the crew chief had stripped Feriha of her shirt and field-dressed the wound. The stray shot had hit her on the clavicle, breaking the bone and redirecting the round through the trapezius muscle and out her back above the scapula. As one man jabbed her with morphine and the other poured on the QuikClot, Shepard had held her hand and talked. He couldn't really remember the gist of what he had said, just that her hand was cold and her pulse weak.

When the Merlin had landed, the medical team were aboard in seconds and had spirited her away. She hadn't regained consciousness during the flight, and he hadn't seen or spoken to her since.

"We identified a body as Dimitri Yegorov," said Porter.

"How'd that go down with the chief?" said Shepard, welcoming the distraction from thinking about the Syrian agent. He sluiced the beer around in the bottle, his eyes coming to rest briefly on his balled up tee shirt and the rosary wrapped in the material at the end of the lounger.

A reminder of the woman who had not been so lucky.

Porter clapped her hand on her thigh.

"Oh, he was cock of the walk taking that to the state department. Between all the dead Russian troops, the intelligence grab and the footage Kestrel brought us, the fires are well and truly lit on the diplomatic front. From what I'm hearing Russian Central Command had been trying to get Yegorov back on the leash for weeks but he'd gone full rogue on them. There's a phone call in to arrange an emergency UN Security Council meeting so you can bet your balls the phones are ringing off the hook from the top down trying to get their excuses in to the Kremlin."

"You got what you wanted then?"

Porter took another sip. Pursed her lips and sighed.

"I don't enjoy this, Tom."

"No?"

"I know you think they're just assets to me, but I care about what happens to people like Feriha. We need people like her, willing to make the hard choices and the sacrifices. At the end of the day, it's their country. We're going to need them when the time finally comes to putting it back on its feet."

Shepard didn't doubt her sincerity or her belief in her argument of it, but he knew that particular goal remained a long way off and in the meantime, men like him and women like Feriha Najir would be pawns in the game of others.

He thought of her again. Lying in the cot hooked up to monitors and medication. Frail, afraid, unsure of where the outcome of her bravery had left her and what her actions had cost. A life. Love. Family. She was alone amongst strangers save for him, after giving her all for people she didn't know.

He looked out over the apron to where a pair of AH-64 Apaches were spinning up for another flight. The mission continued. Another day. Another fight.

He resolved then to finish his beer and visit the med centre. A friendly face was the least she deserved.

"She had the heart of a lion, Porter. You make sure when

all this is done she's looked after."

The CIA agent nodded once. An honest yet unspoken promise.

"The intel you snatched is under review, but some significant pieces are starting to fall into place," she said after a pause.

"Yeah?"

"There are bills of lading and customs stamps tracking back to a shipping company based in Tunis. The precursors that were brought in to weaponise the warheads and the barrel bombs are being analysed by our people. It's early days but the chemicals seem to originate from two factories along the Black Sea Coast."

"Russians again?"

"Maybe, but some stuff originates in Tbilisi. Task Force Falcon already has a face in the frame. He's a money man, but it looks like he's the person to see if you've the desire to get your mitts on the nasties and the cash to pay for it."

"Anything about a manufacturing plant?"

"We've a few leads. Once we've worked them up, I'll speak to McPeak. I'd like Trident to do the raid, but that might not be possible."

Shepard cocked his head. A smile played in the corners of her eyes. She was toying with him. Dangling the carrot. She was good. Although their relationship had been turbulent and fraught of late, Christmas Porter knew men like Shepard were men of action; never happy in dry dock, and even worse when they found themselves adrift on the doldrums of injury or recuperation. There was nothing like the promise of action to speed up the healing process.

Shepard pointed to his arm.

"I'm not much use as a scalpel like this. Can you give me a week or two?"

Christmas Porter rolled her eyes and raised her bottle.

"If you promise not to go solo again."

Shepard gave her a tight smile, but no assurances.

"What about the munitions?" he said.

"Colonel Enders and a team of CNBC specialists have been put on the ground to secure the compound and make sure the chemicals are transported back here and then flown on for full analysis and destruction. Mullah Shami's men have been assisting in the clear up."

"They were a fierce bunch of boys."

"I heard the same was said about you."

Shepard turned around to face her. He could see his beat-up reflection in her Ray-Bans; a split across the bridge of his nose, one black eye and a cut lip, his skin peppered with shrapnel grazes.

The sun caught behind her in a white halo as Porter reached up to take off the glasses and shake out her hair.

Coyote Four and Nine thundered along the tarmac and then leapt into the air, a wash of sand and heat as the rotor wash passed across Shepard's small sunbathing area in the lee of the SOAR hangar.

"Jesus, Porter. You almost made that sound like a compliment."

"Maybe it was."

She raised her bottle and Shepard clicked his own against it.

"So, I guess I didn't do too bad for a bricklayer dressed up as a brain surgeon then?"

Afterword

THANK-YOU FOR READING 'AGENT IN PLACE'

I sincerely hope you enjoyed this Mission-File. If you can **please** spare a moment to leave a review it will be very much appreciated and helps immensely in assisting others to find this, and my other books.

Follow the exploits of Tom Shepard after his Tour of Duty in my Debut novel:

'CODE OF SILENCE'

You can find out about this book and more in the series by signing up at my website:

www.pwjordanauthor.com

Also by Phillip Jordan

COMING SOON- THE BELFAST CRIME SERIES

CODE OF SILENCE
THE CROSSED KEYS
NO GOING BACK

THE BELFAST CRIME CASE-FILES

BEHIND CLOSED DOORS
COMING SOON- INTO THIN AIR

THE TASK FORCE TRIDENT MISSION FILES

AGENT IN PLACE
COMING SOON- DOUBLE CROSS

Get Exclusive Material

GET EXCLUSIVE NEWS AND UPDATES FROM THE AUTHOR

Building a relationship with my readers is *the* best thing about writing.

Visit and join up for information on new books and deals and to find out more about my life growing up on the same streets as Tom Shepard, you will receive the exclusive e-book 'IN/FAMOUS' containing an in-depth interview and a selection of True Crime stories about the flawed but fabulous city that inspired me to write.

You can get this **for free,** by signing up at my website.

Visit at www.pwjordanauthor.com

About Phillip Jordan

ABOUT PHILLIP JORDAN

Phillip Jordan was born in Belfast, Northern Ireland and grew up in the city that holds the dubious double honour of being home to Europe's Most Bombed Hotel and scene of its largest ever bank robbery.
He had a successful career in the Security Industry for twenty years before transitioning into the Telecommunications Sector.
Aside from writing Phillip has competed in Olympic and Ironman Distance Triathlon events both Nationally and Internationally including a European Age-Group Championship and the World Police and Fire Games.
Taking the opportunity afforded by recent world events to write full-time Phillip wrote his Debut Crime Thriller, CODE OF SILENCE, finding inspiration in the dark and tragic history of Northern Ireland but also in the black humour, relentless tenacity and Craic of the people who call the fabulous but flawed City of his birth home.

Phillip now lives on the County Down coast and is currently writing two novel series.
For more information:

www.pwjordanauthor.com
www.facebook.com/phillipjordanauthor/

Copyright

A FIVE FOUR PUBLICATION.
First published in Great Britain in 2020
FIVE FOUR PUBLISHING LIMITED
Copyright © 2020 PHILLIP JORDAN

The moral right of Phillip Jordan to be identified as the author of this work has been asserted by him in accordance with the Copyright, Designs and Patents Act 1988.

All the characters and events in this book are fictitious, and any resemblance to actual entities or persons either living or dead is purely coincidental.

All rights reserved. No part of this publication may be reproduced, stored in a retrieval system or transmitted in any form or by any means, without prior permission in writing of the publisher, nor to be otherwise circulated in any form of binding or cover other than that in which it is published without a similar condition, including this condition, being imposed on the subsequent purchaser.

Cover Image- Shutterstock

* * *

FIVE FOUR PUBLISHING

Printed in Great Britain
by Amazon